CIRCLE OF GOLD

**Center Point
Large Print**

**This Large Print Book carries the
Seal of Approval of N.A.V.H.**

DIANA PALMER

CIRCLE OF GOLD

Center Point Publishing
Thorndike, Maine

This Center Point Large Print edition
is published in the year 2005 by arrangement with
Harlequin Enterprises Ltd.

The text of this Large Print edition is unabridged.
In other aspects, this book may vary from the original edition.
Printed in Thailand. Set in 16-point Times New Roman type.

ISBN 1-58547-521-1

Library of Congress Cataloging-in-Publication Data

Palmer, Diana.
   Circle of gold / Diana Palmer.--Center Point large print ed.
     p. cm.
   ISBN 1-58547-521-1 (lib. bdg. : alk. paper)
    1. Secretaries--Fiction. 2. Single fathers--Fiction. 3. Ranchers--Fiction. 4. Large
type books. I. Title.

PS3566.A513C57 2004
813'.54--dc22

                                                                              2004013323

CIRCLE OF GOLD

Chapter 1

Kasie Mayfield was excited. Her gray eyes were brimming with delight as she sat in the sprawling living room at the Double C Ranch in Medicine Ridge, Montana. There was a secretarial position available on the mammoth Double C, and she had the necessary qualifications. She was only twenty-two, but she had a certificate from secretarial school and plenty of initiative. Besides all that, the position was secretary to John Callister, the second son of the well-known family that headed not only a publishing empire in New York City, but a cattle empire out West.

There was a very interesting story about the ranch in a magazine that Kasie was reading while she waited her turn to be interviewed. The elder Callisters lived in New York, where they published, among others, a famous sports magazine. When they weren't in the city, they lived in Jamaica on an ancestral estate. The Callister who had founded the American branch of the family had been a British duke. He bought an obscure little magazine in New York City in 1897 and turned it into a publishing conglomerate. One of his sons had emigrated to Montana and founded the ranch. It eventually passed to Douglas Callister, who had raised the boys, Gilbert and John. Nobody talked about why the uncle had been given custody of both boys and left them the ranch when he died. Presumably it was some dark family secret. Apparently there wasn't a lot of contact between the boys and their parents.

Gilbert, the eldest at thirty-two, had been widowed three years ago. He had two young daughters, Bess, who was five, and Jenny, who was four. John had never married. He was a rodeo champion and did most of the traveling that accompanied showing the ranch's prizewinning pedigree black Angus bulls. Gil was the power in the empire. He was something of a marketing genius, and he dealt with the export business and sat on the boards of two multinational corporations. But mostly he ran the ranch, all thirty thousand acres of it.

There was a photograph of him in the magazine, but she didn't need it to know what he looked like. Kasie had gotten a glimpse of him on her way into the house to wait for her turn to be interviewed. One glimpse had been enough. It shocked her that a man who didn't even know her should glare at her so intently.

A more conceited woman might have taken it for masculine interest. But Kasie had no ego. No, that tall, lanky blond man hadn't liked her, and made no secret of it. His pale blue eyes under that heavy brow had pierced her skin. She wouldn't get the job. He'd make sure of it.

She glanced at the woman next to her, a glorious blonde with big brown eyes and beautiful legs crossed under a thigh-high skirt. Then she looked at her own ankle-length blue jumper with a simple gray blouse that matched her big eyes. Her chestnut hair was in a long braid down her back. She wore only a little lipstick on her full, soft mouth, and no rouge at all on her cheeks. She had a rather ordinary oval face and a small, rounded chin, and she wore contact lenses. She wasn't at all pretty. She had a nice figure, but she was shy and didn't make the most of it. It was just as well that she had good office skills, she supposed, because it was highly unlikely that anybody would ever want to actually marry her. She thought of her parents and her brother and had to fight down tears. It was so soon. Too soon, probably. But the job might keep her from thinking of what had happened. . . .

"Miss Mayfield!"

She jumped as her name was called in a deep, authoritative tone. "Yes?"

"Come in, please."

She put a smile on her face as she clutched her small purse in her hands and walked into the paneled office, where plaques and photos of bulls lined the walls and burgundy leather furniture surrounded the big mahogany desk. A man was sitting there, with his pale eyes piercing and intent. A blond man with broad shoulders and a hard, lean face that seemed to be all rocky edges. It was not John Callister.

She stopped in front of the desk with her heart pounding and didn't bother to sit down. Gil Callister was obviously doing the interviews, and now she was sure she wouldn't get the job. She knew John Callister from the drugstore where she'd worked briefly as a stock clerk putting herself through secretarial courses. John had talked to her, teased her and even told her about the secretarial job. He'd have given her a chance. Gil would just shoot her out the door. It was obvious that he didn't like anything about her.

He tossed a pen onto the desk and nodded toward the chair facing it. "Sit down."

She felt vulnerable. The door was closed. Here she was with a hungry tiger, and no way out. But she sat anyway. Never let it be said that she lacked courage. They could throw her into the arena and she would die like a true Roman . . . She shook herself. She really had to stop reading the Plinys and Tacitus. This was the new millennium, not the first century A.D.

"Why do you want this job?" Gil asked bluntly.

Her thin eyebrows lifted. She hadn't expected the question. "Because John is a dish?" she ventured dryly.

The answer seemed to surprise him. "Is he?"

"When I worked at the drugstore, he was always kind to me," she said evasively. "He told me about the job, because he knew I was just finishing my secretarial certificate at the vocational-technical school. I got high grades, too."

Gil pursed his lips. He still didn't smile. He looked down at the résumé she'd handed him and read it carefully, as if he was looking for a deficiency he could use to deny her the job. His mouth made a thin line. "Very high grades," he conceded with obvious reluctance. "This is accurate? You really can type 110 words a minute?"

She nodded. "I can type faster than I can take dictation, actually."

He pushed the résumé aside and leaned back. "Boyfriends?"

She was nonplussed. Her fingers tightened on her purse. "Sir?"

"I want to know if you have any entanglements that might cause you to give up the job in the near future," he persisted, and seemed oddly intent on the reply.

She shifted restlessly. "I've only ever had one real boyfriend, although he was more like a brother. He married my best friend two months ago. That was just before I moved to Billings," she added, mentioning the nearby city, "to live with my aunt. So, I don't date much."

She was so uncomfortable that she almost squirmed. He didn't know about her background, of course, or he wouldn't need to ask such questions. Modern women were a lot more worldly than Kasie. But she'd said that John was a dish. She flushed. Good grief, did he think she went around seducing men or something? Was that why he didn't want her in his house? Her expression was mortified.

He averted his eyes. "You have some odd character references," he said after a minute, frowning at them. "A Catholic priest, a nun, a Texas Ranger and a self-made millionaire with alleged mob ties."

She only smiled demurely. "I have unique friend-ships."

"You could put it that way," he said, diverted. "Is the millionaire your lover?"

She went scarlet and her jaw dropped.

"Oh, hell, never mind," he said, apparently disturbed that he'd asked the question and uncomfortable at the reaction it drew. "That's none of my business.

All right, Kasie . . ." He hesitated. "Kasie. What's it short for?"

"I don't know," she blurted out. "It's my actual name."

One eye narrowed. "The millionaire's name is K.C.," he pointed out. "And he's at least forty."

"Thirty-seven. He saved my mother's life, while she was carrying me," she said finally. "He wasn't always a millionaire."

"Yes, I know, he was a professional soldier, a mercenary." His eyes narrowed even more. "Want to tell me about it?"

"Not really, no," she confided.

He shook his head. "Well, if nothing else, you'll be efficient. You're also less of a distraction than the rest of them. There's nothing I hate more than a woman who wears a skirt up to her briefs to work and then complains when men stare at her if she bends over. We have dress codes at our businesses and they're enforced—for both sexes."

"I don't have any skirts that come up to my . . . well, I don't wear short ones," she blurted out.

"So I noticed," he said with a deliberate glance at her long dress.

She fumbled with her purse while he went over the résumé one last time. "All right, Kasie, you can start Monday at eight-thirty. Did John tell you that the job requires you to live here?"

"No!"

His eyebrows arched. "Not in his room, of course," he added just to irritate her, and then looked satisfied when she blushed. "Miss Parsons, who has charge of my daughters, lives in. So does Mrs. Charters who does the cooking and housekeeping. We have other part-time help that comes infrequently. Board and meals are provided by us, in addition to your salary." He named a figure that made Kasie want to hold on to something. It was astronomical compared to what she'd made working at the drugstore part-time. "You'll be a private secretary," he added. "That means you may have to travel with us from time to time."

"Travel?" Her face softened.

"Do you like to travel?" he asked.

"Oh, yes. I loved it when I was little."

She wondered by the look he gave her if he assumed that her parents had been wealthy. He could not know, of course, that they were both deceased.

"Do you want the job?" he asked.

"Yes," she said.

"All right. I'll tell the others they can leave." He got to his feet, elegant and lithe, moving with a grace that was unequaled in Kasie's circle of acquaintances. He opened the office door, thanked the other young women for coming and told them that the position had been filled. There was a shuffle of feet, some murmuring, and the front door closed.

"Come on, Kasie," Gil said. "I'll introduce you to . . ."

"Daddy!" came a wail from the end of the hall. A little girl with disheveled long blond hair came running and threw herself at Gil, sobbing.

He picked her up, and his whole demeanor changed. "What is it, baby?" he asked in the most tender tone

13

Kasie had ever heard. "What's wrong?"

"Me and Jenny was playing with our dollies on the deck and that bad dog came up on the porch and he tried to bite us!"

"Where's Jenny?" he demanded, immediately threatening.

A sobbing little voice answered him as the younger girl came toddling down the hall rubbing her eyes with dirty little fists. She reached up to Gil, and he picked her up, too, oblivious to her soiled dress and hands.

"Nothing's going to hurt my babies. Did the dog bite either of you?" Gil demanded.

"No, Daddy," Bess said.

"Bad doggie!" Jenny sobbed. "Make him go away!"

"Of course I will!" Gil said roughly, kissing little cheeks with a tenderness that made Kasie's heart ache.

A door opened and John Callister came down the hall, looking very unlike the friendly man Kasie knew from the drugstore. His pale eyes were glittering in his lean, dark face, and he looked murderous.

"Are they all right?" he asked Gil, pausing to touch the girls' hair. "It was that mangy cur that Fred Sims insisted on bringing with him when he hired on. I got between it and the girls and it tried to bite me, too. I called Sims up to the house and told him to get rid of it and he won't, so he's fired."

"Here." Gil handed his girls to his brother and started down the hall with quick, measured steps.

John stared after him. "Maybe Sims will make it to his truck before Gil gets him," he murmured. "But I wouldn't bet on it. Are my babies all right?" he asked, kissing their little damp cheeks as the girls clung to either shoulder.

"Bad old doggie," Bess sobbed. "Our Missie never bites people!"

"Missie's a toy collie," John explained to a silent Kasie with a smile. "She lives indoors. Nothing like that vicious dog Sims keeps. We've had trouble from it before, but Sims was so good with horses that we put up with it. Not any more. We can't let it endanger the girls."

"If it would come right up on the porch and try to bite them, it doesn't need to be around children," Kasie agreed.

The girls looked at her curiously.

"Who are you?" Bess asked.

"I'm Kasie," she replied with a smile. "Who are you?"

"I'm Bess," the child replied. "That's Jenny. She's just four," she added, indicating the smaller child, whose hair was medium-length and more light brown than blond.

"I'm very glad to meet you both," Kasie said, smiling warmly. "I'm going to be Mr. Callister's secretary," she added with an apologetic glance at John. "Sorry."

"Why are you sorry?" John asked amusedly. "I only flog secretaries during full moons."

Her eyes crinkled with merriment and she grinned.

"Gil won't let me hire secretaries because I have such a bad track record," John confessed. "The last one turned out to be a jewel thief. You, uh, don't like jewels?" he added deliberately.

She chuckled. "Only costume jewelry. And unless you wear it, we shouldn't have a problem."

There was a commotion outside and John grimaced. "He'll come back in bleeding, as usual," he muttered. "I just glare at people. Gil hits." He gave Kasie a wicked grin. "Sometimes he hits me, too."

The girls giggled. "Oh, Uncle Johnny," Bess teased, "Daddy never hits you! He won't even hit us. He says little children shouldn't be hitted."

"Hit," Kasie corrected absently.

"Hit," Bess parroted, and grinned. "You're nice."

"You're nice, too, precious," Kasie said, reaching out to smooth back the disheveled hair. "You've got tangles."

"Can you make my hair like yours?" Bess asked, eyeing Kasie's braid. "And tie it with a pink ribbon?"

The opening of the back door stopped the conversation dead. Gil came back in with his shirt and jeans dusty and a cut at the corner of his mouth. As he came closer, wiping away the blood, his bruised and lacerated knuckles became visible.

"So much for that little problem," he said with cold satisfaction. His eyes were still glittery with temper until he looked at the little girls. The anger drained out of him and he smiled. "Dirty chicks," he chided. "Go get Miss Parsons to clean you up."

John put them down and Bess looked up at her father accusingly. "Miss Parsons don't like little kids."

"Go on. If she gives you any trouble, come tell me," Gil told the girls.

"Okay, Daddy!"

Bess took Jenny's hand and, with a shy grin at Kasie, she drew the other child with her up the winding staircase.

"They like Kasie already," John commented. "Bess said . . ."

"Miss Parsons takes care of the kids," Gil said shortly. "Show Kasie the way we keep records. She's a computer whiz in addition to her dictation skills. She should be able to get all those herd records onto diskettes for you. Then we can get rid of the paper clutter before we end up buried in it."

"Okay," John said. He hesitated. "Sims get off okay?"

"Sure," Gil said easily. "No problem." He wiped the blood away from his mouth with a wicked look at his brother before he turned and went up the staircase after the children.

John just shook his head. "Never mind. Come on, Kasie. Let's get you started."

Kasie moved into the house that weekend. Most of her parents' things, and her own, were at Mama Luke's, about ten miles away in Billings, Montana, to whom she'd come for refuge after losing her family. She had only the bare necessities of clothing and personal items; it barely filled one small suitcase. When she walked into the ranch house with it, Gil was on the porch with one of his men. He gave her a curious appraisal, dismissing the man.

17

"Where's the rest of your stuff?" he asked, glancing past her at the small, white used car she drove, which she'd parked beside the big garage. "In the trunk?"

"This is all the stuff I have," she said.

He looked stunned. "Surely you have furniture . . . ?"

"My other things are at my aunt's house. But I don't have much stuff of my own."

He stepped aside to let her go inside, his face curious and his eyes intent on her. He didn't say a word, but he watched her even more closely from then on.

The first week on the job, she lost a file that Gil needed for a meeting he was flying to in the family Piper plane. It was an elegant aircraft, twin-engine and comfortable. Gil and John could both fly it and did, frequently, trucking the livestock they were showing from one state to the next with employees. Kasie wished she could go with the livestock, right now. Gil was eloquent about the missing file, his deep voice soft and filled with impatience.

"If you'll just be quiet for a minute, Mr. Callister, I'll find it!" she exclaimed finally, driven to insubordination.

He gave her a glare, but he shut up. She rustled through the folders on her desk with cold, nervous hands. But she did find the file. She extended it, sheepishly, grimacing at the look in his eyes.

"Sorry," she added hopefully.

It didn't do any good. His expression was somber and half-angry. His eyes glittered down at her. She thought absently that he looked very nice in a gray vested suit. It suited his fair hair and light eyes and his nice tan. It also emphasized the excellent fitness of his tall, muscular body. Kasie thought idly that he must have women practically stalking him when he went to dinner meetings. He was striking just to look at, in addition to that very masculine aura that clung to him like his expensive cologne.

"Where's John?" he asked.

"He had a date," she said. "I'm trying to cope with the new tax format."

His eyes narrowed. "Surely they taught tax compilation at your school?"

She grimaced. "Well, actually, they didn't. It's a rather specialized skill."

"Buy what you need from the bookstore or the computer store and have them send me the bill," he said shortly. "If you can't cope, tell me that, too."

She didn't dare. She wouldn't have a job, and she had to support herself. She couldn't expect Mama Luke to do it. "I can cope, sir," she assured him.

His eyes narrowed as he stared down at her. "One thing more," he added curtly. "My girls are Miss Parsons' responsibility, not yours."

"I only read them a story," she began, blushing guiltily.

His eyebrows arched. "I was referring to the way you braided Bess's hair," he said. "I thought it was an isolated incident."

She swallowed. Hardly isolated. The girls were always somewhere close by when Kasie stopped for lunch or her breaks. She shared her desserts with the children and frequently read to them or took them on walks to point out the various sorts of flowers and trees around the ranch house. Gil didn't know that and she'd hoped the girls hadn't said anything. Miss Parsons was curt and bullying with the children, whom she obviously disliked. It was inevitable that they'd turn to Kasie, who adored them.

"Only one story," she lied.

He seethed. "In case you didn't get the message the first time, Kasie, I am not in the market for a wife or a mother for my daughters."

The insult made her furious. She glared up at him, forgetting all her early teachings about turning cheeks and humility. "I came to work here because I need a job," she said icily. "I'm only twenty-two, Mr. Callister," she added. "And I don't have any interest in a man almost old enough to be my father, with a ready-made family to boot!"

His reaction was unexpected. He didn't fire back. He grew very quiet. He turned and went out of the room without another word. A minute later, she heard the front door close and, soon, an engine fire up.

"So there," she added to herself.

Gil came home from his trip even quieter than when he'd left. There was tension between him and Kasie, because she hadn't forgotten the insulting remark he'd made to her before he left. As if she'd come to work here just so she could chase him. Really! But there was another complication now, as well. Kasie was a nervous wreck trying to keep him from seeing how much time she actually spent with his little girls. She didn't need to worry when he was off on his frequent business trips, but they suddenly stopped. He started sending Brad Dalton, his manager, to seminars and conferences. He stayed home on the pretext of overseeing massive improvements on the property.

It was just after roundup, when the cattle business was taking up a little less of his time. But there were new bunkhouses being built, as well as new wells being dug in the pastures and new equipment brought in for tagging and vaccinations of new calves. The trucks were being overhauled, along with the other farm machinery such as tractors and combines that harvested the grain crops. The barns were repaired, a new silo erected. It was a busy time.

Kasie found herself involved unexpectedly with Gil when John went out of state to show two new bulls at a pedigree competition and Gil's secretary, Pauline Raines, conveniently sprained her thumb and couldn't type.

"I need these yesterday," he said without preamble, laying a thick sheaf of papers beside Kasie's neat little hand on the desk. "Pauline can't do them. She missed the tennis ball and hit her thumb with the tennis racket."

She managed not to make a disparaging comment— barely. She didn't like Pauline any more than Gil's daughters did. The woman was lazy and seductive, and always hanging on Gil like a tie. What little work she actually did was of poor quality and she was pitifully slow as well. She worked at the ranch office near the front of the house three days a week, and Kasie had already inherited a good deal of her work. Pauline spent her time by the pool when Gil wasn't watching. Now, Kasie thought miserably, she was going to end up doing not only John's paperwork, including the unbelievably complex taxes that she was still struggling to understand, but Gil's as well.

"I don't guess she could type with her toes?" she murmured absently.

There was an odd sound, but when she looked up, Gil's hard face was impassive. "How long will it take?" he persisted.

She looked at the pages. They weren't data, as she'd first thought, but letters to various stock producers. They all had different headings, but the same basic body. "Is this all?" she asked with cool politeness.

He glowered at her. "There are fifty of them. They'll have to be done individually . . ."

"No, they won't," she said gently. "All you have to do—" she opened a new file, selected the option she needed and began typing "—is type the body of the letter once and then just type the various addresses and combine them. An hour's work."

He looked as if he'd been slapped. "Excuse me?"

"This word processor does all that for you," she explained. "It's very simple, really."

He looked angry. "I thought you had to type all fifty individually."

"Only if you're using a prehistoric typewriter and carbon system," she pointed out.

He was really angry now. "An hour?" he repeated.

She nodded. "Maybe less. I'll get right on it," she added quickly, hoping to appease him. Heaven only knew what had set him off, but she recognized that glitter in his eyes.

He left her and went to make some phone calls. When he came back, Kasie was printing the letters out, having just finished the mailing labels. There was a folding machine that made short work of folding the letters. Then all she had to do was stuff, lick, stamp and mail the envelopes.

Gil put on the stamps for her. He watched her curiously. Once, when she looked up into his eyes, it was like an electric shock. Surprised, she dropped her gaze and blushed. Really, she thought, he had a strange effect on her.

"How do you like your job so far?" he asked.

"Very much," she said. "Except for the taxes."

"You'll get used to doing them," he assured her.

"I suppose so."

"Can you manage John's load and mine as well, or do you want me to get a temporary to help you?"

"There isn't a lot," she pointed out. "If I get overwhelmed, I'll say so."

He finished stamping the envelopes and stacked them neatly to one side. "You're very honest. It's unusual in most people." He touched a stamp with a floral motif. "My wife was like that." He smiled. "She said that lies were a waste of time, since they got found out anyway." His eyes were far away. "We were in grammar school together. We always knew that

23

we'd marry one day." The smile faded into misery. "She was a wonderful rider. She rode in the rodeo when she was younger. But a gentle horse ran away with her and a low-lying limb ended her life. Jenny was only a year old when Darlene died. Bess was two. I thought my life was over, too."

Kasie didn't know what to say. It shocked her that a man like Gil would even discuss something so personal with a stranger. Of course, a lot of people discussed even more personal things with Kasie. Maybe she had that sort of face that attracted confidences.

"Do the girls look like her?" she asked daringly.

"Bess does. She was blond and blue-eyed. She wasn't beautiful, but her smile was." His eyes narrowed in painful memory. "They had to sedate me to make me let go of her. I wouldn't believe them, even when they swore to me that no means on earth could save her . . ." His fingers clenched on top of the envelope and he moved his hand away at once and stood up. "Thanks, Kasie," he said curtly, turning away, as if it embarrassed him to have spoken of his wife at all.

"Mr. Callister," she said softly, waiting until he turned to continue. "I lost . . . some people three months ago. I understand grief."

He hesitated. "How did they die?"

Her face closed up. "It was . . . an accident. They were only in their twenties. I thought they had years left."

"Life is unpredictable," he told her. "Sometimes unbearable. But everything passes. Even bad times."

"Yes, that's what everyone says," she agreed.

They shared a long, quiet, puzzling exchange of sorrow before he shrugged and turned away, leaving her to her work.

Chapter 2

Kasie was almost tearing her hair out by the next afternoon. John's mail was straightforward, mostly about show dates and cancellations, transportation for the animals and personal correspondence. Gil's was something else.

Gil not only ran the ranch, but he dealt with the majority of the support companies that were its satellites. He knew all the managers by first names, he often spoke with state and federal officials, including well-known senators, on legislation affecting beef production. Besides that, he was involved in the scientific study of new grasses and earth-friendly pesticides and fertilizers. He worked with resource and conservation groups, even an animal rights group; since he didn't run slaughter cattle and was rabidly proconservation, at least one group was happy to have his name on its board of directors. He was a powerhouse of energy, working from dawn until well after dark. The problem was, every single task he undertook was accompanied by a ton of paperwork. And his part-time secretary, Pauline Raines, was the most disorganized human being Kasie had ever encountered.

John came home late on Friday evening, and was surprised to find Kasie still at work in the study.

He scowled as he tossed his Stetson onto a rack. "What are you doing in here? It's almost ten o'clock! Does Gil know you're working this much overtime?"

She glanced up from the second page of ten that she was trying to type into the computer. None of Pauline's paperwork had ever been keyed in.

She held up the sheaf of paperwork in six files with a sigh. "I think of it as job security," she offered.

He moved around beside the desk and looked over what she was doing. "Good God, he's not sane!" he muttered. "No one secretary could handle this load in a week! Is he trying to kill you?"

"Pauline hurt her thumb," she said miserably. "I get to do her work, too, except that she never put any of the records into the computer. It's got to be done. I don't see how your brother ever found anything in here!"

"He didn't," John said dryly, his pale eyes twinkling. "Pauline made sure of it. She's indispensable, I hear."

Kasie's eyes narrowed. "She won't be for long, when I get this stuff keyed in," she assured him.

"Don't tell her that unless you pay up your life insurance first. Pauline is a girl who carries grudges, and she's stuck on Gil."

"I noticed."

"Not that he cares," John added slowly. "He never got over losing his wife. I'm not sure that he'll ever remarry."

"He told me."

He glanced down at her. "Excuse me?"

"He told me specifically that he didn't want a mother for the girls or a new wife, and not to get my hopes up." She chuckled. "Good Lord, he must be all of thirty-two. I'm barely twenty-two. I don't want a man I'll have to push around in a wheelchair one day!"

"And I don't rob cradles," came a harsh, angry voice from the doorway.

They both jumped as they looked up to see Gil just coming in from the barn. He was still in work clothes, chaps and boots and a sweaty shirt, with a disreputable old black Stetson cocked over one eye.

"Are you trying to make Kasie quit, by any chance?" John challenged. "Good God, man, it'll take her a week just to get a fraction of the information in these spreadsheets into the computer!"

Gil frowned. He pulled off his hat and ran a hand through his sweaty blond hair. "I didn't actually look at it," he confessed. "I've been too busy with the new bulls."

"Well, you'd better look," John said curtly.

Gil moved to the desk, aware of Kasie's hostile glare. He peered over her shoulder and cursed sharply. "Where did all this come from?" he asked.

"Pauline brought it to me and said you wanted it converted to disk," she replied flatly.

His eyes began to glitter. "I never told her to land you with all this!"

"It needs doing," she confessed. "There's no way you can do an accurate spreadsheet without the comparisons you could use in a computer program. I've

27

reworked this spreadsheet program," she said, indicating the screen, "and made an application that will work for cattle weight gain ratios and daily weighing, as well as diet and health and so forth."

"I'm impressed," Gil said honestly.

"It's what I'm used to doing. Taxes aren't," she added sheepishly.

"Don't look at me," John said. "I hate taxes. I'm not learning them, either," he added belligerently. "Half this ranch is mine, and on my half, we don't do tax work." He nodded curtly and walked out.

"Come back here, you coward!" Gil muttered. "How the hell am I supposed to cope with taxes and all the other routine headaches that you don't have, because you're off somewhere showing cattle!"

John just waved his hand and kept walking.

"Miss Parsons knows taxes inside out," Kasie ventured. "She told me she used to be an accountant."

He glared at her. "Miss Parsons was hired to take care of my daughters." He kept looking at Kasie, and not in any friendly way. It was almost as if he knew . . .

She flushed. "They couldn't get the little paper ship to float on the fishpond," she murmured uneasily, not looking at him. "I only helped."

"And fell in the pond."

She grimaced. "I tripped. Anybody can trip!" she added in a challenging tone, her gray eyes flashing at him.

"Over their own feet?" he mused.

Actually it had been over Bess's stuffed gorilla. The

thing was almost her size and Kasie hadn't realized it was there. The girls had laughed and then wailed, thinking she'd be angry at them. Miss Parsons had fussed for hours when Bess got dirt on her pretty yellow dress. But Kasie didn't scold. She laughed, and the girls were so relieved, she could have cried. They really didn't like Miss Parsons.

He put both hands on his lean hips and studied her with reluctant interest. "The girls tell me everything, Kasie," he said finally. He didn't add that the girls worshiped this quiet, studious young woman who didn't even flirt with John, much less the cowboys who worked for the family. "I thought I'd made it perfectly clear that I didn't want you around them."

She took her hands off the keyboard and looked up at him with wounded eyes. "Why?"

The question surprised him. He scowled, trying to think up a fair answer. Nothing came to mind, which made him even madder.

"I don't have any ulterior motives," she said simply. "I like the girls very much, and they like me. I don't understand why you don't want me to associate with them. I don't have a bad character. I've never been in trouble in my life."

"I didn't think you had," he said angrily.

"Then why can't I play with them?" she persisted. "Miss Parsons is turning them into little robots. She won't let them play because they get dirty, and she won't play with them because it isn't dignified. They're miserable."

"Discipline is a necessary part of childhood," he

said curtly. "You spoil them."

"For heaven's sake, somebody needs to! You're never here," she added shortly.

"Stop right there, while you still have a job," he interrupted, and his eyes made threats. "Nobody tells me how to raise my kids. Especially not some frumpy little backwoods secretary!"

Frumpy? Backwoods? Her eyes widened. She stood up. She was probably already fired, so he could just get it from the hip. "I may be frumpy," she admitted, "and I may be from the backwoods, but I know a lot about little kids! You don't stick them in a closet until they're legal age. They need to be challenged, made curious about the world around them. They need nurturing. Miss Parsons isn't going to nurture them, and Mrs. Charters doesn't have time to. And you aren't ever here at bedtime, even if you're not away on business," she repeated bluntly. "Whole weeks go by when you barely have time to tell them good-night. They need to be read to, so they will learn to love books. They need constructive supervision. What they've got is barbed wire and silence."

His fists clenched by his side, and his expression darkened. She lifted her chin, daring him to do anything.

"You're an expert on children, I guess?" he chided.

"I took care of one," she said, her eyes darkening. "For several months."

"Why did you quit?"

He was assuming that she'd meant a job. She didn't. The answer to his question was a nightmare. She couldn't bear to remember it. "I wasn't suited to the task," she said primly. "But I won't corrupt your little girls by speaking to them."

He was still glowering. He didn't want Kasie to grow close to the girls. He didn't want her any closer to him than a desk and a computer was. His eyes went involuntarily to the desk piled high with Pauline's undone work. The files were supposed to have been converted to computer months earlier, when he'd hired the woman. He'd assumed that it had been done, because she was always ready with the information he needed. He felt suddenly uneasy.

"Check out Black Ribbon's growth information for me," he said suddenly.

She hesitated, but apparently she was still working for him. She sat down and pulled the information up on the computer. He went to his desk and pulled a spreadsheet from a drawer. He brought it to Kasie and had her compare it with the figures she'd just put into the computer. There was a huge difference, to his favor.

He said a word that caused Kasie's face to grow bright red. That disturbed him, but he didn't allude to it. "I've made modifications to improve what seemed like a deficiency in diet. Now it looks as if it wasn't even necessary. How long will it take you to get the breeding herd information transcribed?"

"Well, I've done about a third of it," she said. "But John has letters and information to be compiled for this new show . . ."

"You're mine until we get this information on the

computer. I'll make it all right with John."

"What about Pauline?" she asked worriedly.

"Pauline is my concern, not yours," he told her.

"Okay, boss. Whatever you say."

He made an odd gesture with one shoulder and gave her a long scrutiny. "I told you to let me know if there was too much work. Why didn't you?"

"I thought I could keep up," she said simply. "I wouldn't have complained as long as I could do it within a couple of weeks, and I can."

"Working fourteen-hour shifts," he chided.

"Well, work is work," she said. "I don't mind. It's not as if I have an active social life or an earth-shaking novel to write or anything. And I get paid a duke's ransom as it is."

He frowned. "Why don't you have a social life?"

"Because cowboys stink," she shot right back.

He started to speak, burst out laughing and walked to the door. "Stop that and go to bed. I'll have you some help by morning. Good night, Kasie."

"Good night, Mr. Callister."

He hesitated, turned, studied her, but he didn't speak. He left her tidying up and went upstairs to change out of his work clothes and have a shower.

The next morning, when she went into the office, Pauline was there and so was Gil. They stopped talking when Kasie walked in, so she assumed that they'd been talking about her. Apparently it hadn't been in a friendly way. Pauline's delicate features were drawn in anger and Gil's eyes were narrow and glittery.

"It's about time you got down here!" Pauline said icily.

"It's eight twenty-five," Kasie said, taken aback. "I'm not supposed to be in here until eight-thirty."

"Well, let's get started, then," Pauline said, flopping down at the computer.

"Doing what, exactly?" Kasie asked, disconcerted.

"Teach her how to put information on the computer," Gil said in a voice that didn't invite argument. "And while she's doing that, you can tackle John's work."

Kasie grimaced. Her pupil didn't look eager or willing. It was going to be a long morning.

It was, too. Pauline made the job twice as tedious, questioning every keystroke twice and grumbling— when Gil was out of the office—about having to work with Kasie.

"Look, this wasn't my idea," Kasie assured her. "I could do it myself if Mr. Callister would just let me."

Pauline didn't soften an inch. "You're trying to get his attention, playing up to those kids," she accused. "You want him."

Kasie just looked at her. "I love children," she said quietly. "But I don't want to get married."

"Who said anything about marriage?" Pauline chided.

Kasie averted her eyes. "I needed a job and John needed a secretary," she murmured as she turned a spreadsheet page.

33

"Funny. You call him John, but Gil is 'Mr. Callister.' Why?"

The younger woman blinked. "John is just a few years older than I am," she replied.

Pauline frowned. "How old are you?"

"Twenty-two."

There was a long pause. "Well!" she said finally. She pursed her lips and entered a number into the computer. "You think Gil is old, do you?"

"Yes." She didn't, really, but it seemed safer to say so. She did, after all, have to work with this perfumed barracuda for the immediate future.

Pauline actually smiled. But only for a minute. "What do I do now?" she asked when she finished entering the last number.

Kasie showed her, faintly disturbed by that smile. Oh, well, she'd figure it out later, maybe.

Pauline went home at five o'clock. By now, she had a good idea of how to use the computer. Practice would hone her skills. Kasie wondered why Gil, who had the lion's share of the work, only had a part-time secretary.

When he came back in, late Saturday night, dressed in evening clothes with a black tie and white ruffled shirt, Kasie was still in the office finalizing the spreadsheets. She looked up, surprised at how handsome he was dressed like that. Even if he wasn't really good-looking, he had a natural authority and grace of carriage that made him stand out. Not to mention a physique that many a Holly-

34

wood actor would have coveted.

"I thought I told you to give up this night work," he said curtly.

She spared him a glance while she saved the information onto a diskette. "You won't let me play with the girls. I don't have anything else to do."

"Watch television. We have all the latest movies on pay-per-view. You can watch any you like. Read a book. Take up knitting. Learn Dutch. But," he added with unnatural resentment, "stay out of the office after supper."

"Is that an order?" she asked.

"It damned well is!"

He was absolutely bristling, she thought, frowning as she searched his pale blue eyes. She closed the files and shut down the program, uneasy because he was glowering at her.

She got up, neat and businesslike in her beige pantsuit, with her chestnut hair nicely braided and hanging down her back.

But when she went around the desk to go to the door, he blocked her path. She wasn't used to men this close and she backed up a step, which only made things worse. He was so tall that she wished she were wearing high heels. The top of her head barely came up to his nose.

His pale eyes glittered even more. "Old age isn't contagious," he said with pure venom in his deep voice.

"Sir?"

"And don't call me sir!"

She swallowed. He was spoiling for a fight. She couldn't bear the thought of one. Her early life had been in the middle of a violent battleground, and loud noises and voices still upset her. "Okay," she agreed immediately.

He slammed his hands into his pockets and glared more. "I'm thirty-two. Ten years isn't a generation and I'm not a candidate for Social Security."

"Okay," she repeated uneasily.

"For God's sake, stop agreeing with me!" he snapped.

She started to say "Okay" again, and bit her tongue. She was as rigid as a ruler, waiting for more explosions with her breath trapped in her throat.

He took his hands out of his pockets and they clenched at his sides as he looked down at her with more conflicting emotions than he'd ever felt. She wasn't beautiful, but there was a tenderness in her that he craved. He hadn't had tenderness in his life since Darlene's untimely death. This young woman made him hungry for things he couldn't grasp. He didn't understand it, and it angered him.

Kasie was wavering between a dash for the door or backing up again. "Do you want me to quit?" she blurted out.

His teeth ground together. "Yes."

She swallowed. "All right. I'll leave in the morning." She moved around him to the door, trying not to take it personally. Sometimes people just didn't like other people.

"No!"

His voice stopped her with her hand on the door-knob.

There was a long pause. Kasie turned, surprised by his indecision. From what she already knew of Gil Callister, he wasn't a man who had trouble making decisions. But he seemed divided about Kasie.

She went toward him, noticing the odd expression on his face when she stopped within arm's length and folded her hands at her waist.

"I know you don't like me," she said gently. "It's all right. I'll really try hard to stay away from the girls. Once Pauline learns how to input the computer files, you won't even have to see me."

He seemed troubled now. Genuinely troubled. He sighed as if he were carrying the weight of the world on his shoulders. At that moment, he looked as if he needed comforting.

"Bess would love it if you took her and Jenny to one of those cartoon movies," she said out of the blue. "There's a Sunday matinee at the Twin Oaks Cinema."

He still didn't speak.

She searched his cold eyes. "I'm sorry that I've gone behind your back to spend time with them. It's not what you think. I mean, I'm not trying to worm my way into your family, even if Pauline does think so. The girls . . . remind me . . . of my own little niece." Her voice almost broke but she controlled it quickly.

"Does she live far away?" he asked abruptly.

Her eyes darkened. "Very . . . far away . . . now," she managed. She forced a smile. "I miss her."

She had to turn away then, or lose control of her wild emotions.

"You can stay for the time being," he said finally, reluctantly. "It will work out."

"That's what my aunt always says," she murmured as she opened the door.

"I didn't know you had family. Your parents are dead, aren't they?"

"They died years ago, when I was little. My aunt was in charge of us until we started school."

"Us?"

She couldn't say it, she couldn't, she couldn't. "I ha . . . have a twin brother," she corrected quickly.

She lifted her head, praying for strength. "Good night, Mr. Callister."

She heard the silence of his disapproval, but she was too upset to care. She went up the staircase with no hesitation at all, straight to her room. She locked the door and lay down on the covers, crying silently so that no one would hear.

There was a violent storm that night. The lightning lit up the whole sky. Kasie heard engines starting up and men's voices yelling. The animals must be unsettled. She'd read that cattle didn't like lightning.

She got up to look out the window, and then she heard the urgent knocking at her door.

She went to it, still in her neat thick white cotton gown that concealed the soft lines of her body. Her hair was loose down her back, disheveled, and she was barely awake.

She opened the door, and looked down. There were Bess and Jenny with tears streaming down their faces. Bess was clutching a small teddy bear, and Jenny had her blanket.

"Oh, my babies, what's wrong?" she asked softly, going down on her knees to pull them close and cuddle them.

"The sky's making an awful noise, Kasie, and we're scared," Bess said.

She threw caution to the winds. She was already in so much trouble, surely a little more wouldn't matter.

"Do you want to climb in with me?" she asked softly.

"Can we?" Bess asked.

"Of course. Come on."

They climbed into bed with her and under the covers, Jenny on one side and Bess on the other.

"Want a story," Jenny murmured.

"Me, too," Bess seconded.

"Okay. How about the three bears?"

"No, Kasie, that's scary," Bess said. "How about the mouse and the lion?"

"Aren't you scared of lions?" she asked the girls.

"We like lions," Bess told her contentedly, cuddling closer. "Daddy took us to the zoo and we saw lions and tigers and polar bears!"

"The lion it is, then."

And she proceeded to tell them drowsily about the mouse who took out the thorn in the lion's paw and made a friend for life. By the time she finished, they were both asleep. She kissed their pretty little sleeping faces and folded them close to her as the lightning flashed and the thunder rolled. She wondered just before she fell asleep how much trouble she'd be in if their father came home and found them with her, after she'd just promised not to play with them. If only, she thought, Gilbert Callister would get a thorn in his paw and she could pull it out and make friends with him. . . .

It was almost two in the morning when Gil and John got back from the holding pens. There had been a stampede, and two hundred head of cattle broke through their fences and spilled out into the pasture that fronted on a highway. The brothers and every hand on the place were occupied for three hours working in the violent storm to round them up and get them back into the right pasture and fix the fence. It helped that the lightning finally stopped, and in its wake came a nice steady rain. But everyone was soaked by the time they finished, and eager for a warm, dry bed.

Gil stripped off his wet clothes and took a shower, wrapping a long burgundy silk robe around his tall body before he went to check on the girls. He opened the door to the big room they shared and his heart skipped a beat when he realized they were missing.

Where in hell was Miss Parsons and where were his children? He went along to her room and almost knocked at the door, when he realized suddenly where the girls were most likely to be.

With his lips making a thin line, he went along the corridor barefoot to Kasie's room. Without knocking, he opened the door and walked in. Sure enough, curled up as close as they could get to her, were Bess and Jenny.

He started to wake them up and insist that they go back to bed, when he saw the way they looked.

It had been a long time since he'd seen their little faces so content. Without a mother—despite the housekeeper and Miss Parsons—they were sad so much of the time. But when they were around Kasie, they changed. They smiled. They laughed. They played. He couldn't remember the last time he'd seen them so happy. Was it fair to deny them Kasie's company just because he didn't like her? On the other hand, was it wise to let them get so attached to her when she might quit or he might fire her?

The question worried him. As he pondered the situation, Kasie moved and the cover fell away from her sleeping form. He moved closer to the bed in the dim light from the security lights outside, and abruptly he realized that she was wearing the sort of gown a dowager might. It was strictly for utility, plain and white, with no ruffles or lace or even a fancy border. He scowled. Kasie was twenty-two. Was it normal for a woman her age to be so repressed that she covered herself from head to toe even in sleep?

She moved again, restlessly, and a single word broke from her lips as the nightmare came again.

"Kantor," she whispered. "Kantor!"

Chapter 3

Without thinking, Gil reached down and shook Kasie's shoulder. "Wake up, Kasie!" he said firmly.

Her eyes opened on a rush of breath. There was horror in them for a few seconds until she came awake and realized that her boss was standing over her. She blinked away the sleepiness and pulled herself up on an elbow. Her beautiful thick chestnut hair swirled around her shoulders below the high neck of the gown as she stared at him.

"You were having a nightmare," he said curtly. "Who's Kantor?"

She hesitated for a few seconds. "My brother," she said finally. "My twin." She noticed that he was wearing a long robe and apparently nothing under it. Thick dark blond hair was visible in the deep vee of the neckline. She averted her eyes almost in panic. It embarrassed her to have him see her in her nightgown; almost as much as to see him in a robe.

"Why do you have nightmares about him?" he asked gently.

"We had an argument," she said. She pushed back her hair. "I don't want to talk about it."

His eyes narrowed. Apparently it was a painful subject. He let it drop. His eyes went to the girls and not without misgiving. "Why are they in here with you?"

"The storm woke them up. They got scared and

came to me," she said defensively. "I didn't go get them."

He was studying them quietly. His expression was hard, grave, wounded.

"I'm sure they went to look for you first," she began defensively.

His eyes glittered down into hers. "We've had this conversation before. Miss Parsons is supposed to be their governess," he emphasized.

"Miss Parsons is probably snoring her head off," she said curtly. "She sleeps like the dead. Bess had a fever week before last, and she didn't even get up when I woke her and told her about it. She said that a fever never hurt anybody!"

"That was when she had strep and I took her to the doctor," he recalled. "Miss Parsons said she was sick. I assumed that she'd been up in the night with her."

"Dream on."

He glared at her. "I'll excuse it this time," he said, ignoring the reference he didn't like to Miss Parsons and her treatment of Bess. He'd have something to say to the woman about that. "Next time, come and find me if you can't wake Miss Parsons."

She just stared back, silent.

"Did you hear me, Kasie?" he demanded softly.

"All right." She glanced from one side of her to the other. "Do you want to wake them up and carry them back to their own beds?"

He looked furious. "If I do, we'll all be awake the rest of the night. We had cattle get out, and we got soaked trying to get them back in. I'm worn-out. I want to go to sleep."

"Nobody here is stopping you," she murmured.

His pale eyes narrowed. "I should have let you go when you offered to resign," he said caustically.

"There's still time," she pointed out, growing more angry by the minute.

He cursed under his breath, glared at her again and walked out.

The next morning, Kasie woke to soft pummeling little hands and laughing voices.

"Get up, Kasie, get up! Daddy's taking us to the movies today!"

She yawned and curled up. "Not me," she murmured sleepily. "Go get breakfast, babies. Mrs. Charters will feed you."

"You got to come, too!" Bess said.

"I want to sleep," she murmured.

"Daddy, she won't get up!" Bess wailed.

"Oh, yes, she will."

Kasie barely had time to register the deep voice before the covers were torn away and she was lifted bodily out of the bed in a pair of very strong arms.

Shocked, she stared straight into pale blue eyes and felt as if she'd been electrified.

"I'll wake her up," Gil told the girls. "Go down and eat your breakfast."

"Okay, Daddy!"

The girls left gleefully, laughing as they went to the staircase.

"You look like a nun in that gown," Gil remarked as he studied his light burden, aware of her sudden stillness. Her face was very close. He searched it quietly. "And you've got freckles, Kasie, just across the bridge of your nose."

"Put . . . put me down," she said, unnerved by the proximity. She didn't like the sensations it caused to feel his chest right against her bare breasts.

"Why?" he asked. He gazed into her eyes. "You hardly weigh anything." His eyes narrowed as he studied her face thoroughly. "You have big eyes," he murmured. "With little flecks of blue in them. Your face looks more round than oval, especially with your hair down. Your mouth is—" he searched for a word, more touched than he wanted to be by its vulnerability "—full and soft. Half-asleep you don't come across as a fighter. But you are, aren't you?"

Her hands were resting lightly around his neck and she stared at him disconcertedly while she wondered what John or Miss Parsons would say if they walked in unexpectedly to find them in this position.

"You should put me down," she said huskily.

"Don't you like being carried?" he murmured absently.

She shivered as she remembered the last time she'd been carried, by an orderly in the hospital . . .

She pushed at him. "Please."

He set her back down, scowling curiously at the odd pastiness of her complexion. "You're mysterious, Kasie."

"Not really. I'm just sleepy." She folded her arms

over her breasts and flushed. "Could you leave, please, and let me get dressed?"

He watched her curiously. "Why don't you date? And don't hand me any bull about stinking cowboys."

She was reluctant to tell him anything about herself. She was a private person. Her aunt, Mama Luke, always said that people shouldn't worry others with their personal problems. She didn't.

"I don't want to get married, ever."

He really scowled then. "Why?"

She thought of her parents and then of Kantor, and her eyes closed on the pain. "Love hurts too much."

He didn't speak. For an instant, he felt the pain that seemed to rack her delicate features, and he understood it, all too well.

"You loved someone who died," he recalled.

She nodded and her eyes met his. "And so did you."

For an instant, his hard face was completely unguarded. He was vulnerable, mortal, wounded. "Yes."

"It doesn't pass away, like they say, does it?" she asked softly.

"Not for a long time."

He moved a step closer, and this time she didn't back up. Her eyes lifted to his. He slid his big, lean hand into the thick waves of her chestnut hair and enjoyed its silkiness. "Why don't you wear your hair down, like this?"

"It's sinful," she whispered.

"What?"

"When you dress and wear your hair in a way that's meant to tempt men, to try to seduce them, it's sinful," she repeated.

His lips fell open. He didn't know how to answer that. He'd never had a woman, especially a modern woman, say such a thing to him.

"Do you think sex is a sin?" he asked.

"Outside of marriage, it is," she replied simply.

"You don't move with the times, do you?" he asked on an expulsion of breath.

"No," she replied.

He started smiling and couldn't stop. "Oh, boy."

"The girls will be waiting. Are you really taking them to a movie?" she asked.

"Yes." One eye narrowed. "I need to take you to one, too. Something X-rated."

She flushed. "Get out of here and stop trying to corrupt me."

"You're overdue."

"Stop or I'll have Mama Luke come over and lecture you."

He frowned. "Mama Luke?"

"My aunt."

"What an odd name."

She shrugged. "Our whole family runs to odd names."

"I noticed."

She made a face. "I work for you. My private life is my own business."

"You don't have a private life," he said, and smiled tenderly.

47

"I'm a great reader. I love Plutarch and Tacitus and Arrian."

"Good God!"

"There's nothing wrong with ancient history. Things were just as bad then as they are now. All the ancient writers said that the younger generation was headed straight to purgatory and the world was corrupt."

"Arrian didn't."

"Arrian wrote about Alexander the Great," she reminded him. "Alexander's world was in fairly good shape, apparently."

"Arrian wrote about Alexander in the distant past, not his own present." His eyes became soft with affection as he looked at her. "Why don't I like you? There isn't a person in my circle of acquaintances who would even know who Arrian was, much less what he wrote about."

"I don't like you much, either," she shot right back. "But I guess I can stand it if you can."

"I'll have to," he mused. "If I let you walk out, the girls will push me down the staircase and call you back to support them at my funeral."

She shivered abruptly and wrapped her arms around herself. Funeral. Funeral . . .

"Kasie!"

Her somber eyes came up. She was barely breathing. "Don't . . . joke about things like that."

"Kasie, I didn't mean it that way," he began.

She forced a smile. "Of course not. I have to get dressed."

He lifted an eyebrow. "You might as well come as

48

you are. I haven't seen a gown like that since I stayed with my grandmother as a child." He shook his head. "You'd set a lingerie shop back decades if that style caught on."

"It's a perfectly functional gown."

"Functional. Yes. It's definitely functional. And about as seductive as chain mail," he added.

"Good!"

He burst out laughing. "All right, I'm leaving."

He went out, sparing her a last, amused glance before he closed the door.

Kasie dressed in jeans and a dark T-shirt. She put her long hair in a braid and pulled on sneakers. She felt a twinge of guilt because she'd missed so many Sunday sermons in past months. But she couldn't reconcile her pain. It needed more time.

The whole family was at the table when she joined them for breakfast. John gave her a warm smile.

"I hear you had visitors last night," he told Kasie with a mischievous glance at the two little girls, who were wolfing down cereal.

"Yes, I did," Kasie replied with a worried glance that encompassed both Gil and Miss Parsons.

"You should have called me, Miss Mayfield," Miss Penny Parsons said curtly and glanced at Kasie with cold dark eyes. "I take care of the children."

Kasie could have argued that point, but she didn't dare. "Yes, Miss Parsons," she said demurely.

Gil finished his scrambled eggs and lifted his coffee cup to his firm lips. He was wearing slacks and a neat yellow sports shirt that emphasized his muscular arms. He looked elegant even in casual wear, Kasie thought, and remembered suddenly the feel of those strong arms around her. She flushed.

He noticed her sudden color and caught her gaze. She couldn't seem to look away, and he didn't even try to. For a space of seconds, they were fused in some sort of bond, prisoners of a sensual connection that made Kasie's full lips part abruptly. His gaze fell to them and lingered with unexpected hunger.

Kasie dropped her fork onto her plate and jumped at the noise. "Sorry!" she said huskily as she fumbled with the fork.

"Didn't get much sleep last night, did you?" John asked with a smile. "Neither did any of us. About midnight, I thought seriously about giving up cattle ranching and becoming a door-to-door vacuum cleaner salesman."

"I felt the same way," Gil confessed. "We're going to have to put a small line cabin out at the holding pens and keep a man there on stormy nights."

"As long as I'm not on your list of candidates," John told his brother.

"I'll keep that in mind. Bess, don't play with your food, please," he added to the little girl, who was finished with her cereal and was now smearing eggs around the rim of her plate.

"I don't like eggs, Daddy," she muttered. "Do I gotta eat 'em?"

"Of course you do, young lady!" Miss Parsons said curtly. "Every last morsel."

Bess looked tortured.

"Miss Parsons, could you ask Mrs. Charters to see me before she plans the supper menu, please?" Gil asked.

Miss Parsons got up. "I will. Eat those eggs, Bess."

She left. Gil gave his oldest daughter a sign by placing his forefinger across his mouth. He lifted Bess's plate, scraped the eggs onto his, and finished them off before Miss Parsons returned.

"Very good," she said, nodding approvingly at Bess's plate. "I told you that you'd grow accustomed to a balanced breakfast. We must keep our bodies healthy. Come on, now, girls. We'll have a nice nap until your father's ready to go to the movies."

Bess grimaced, but she didn't protest. She got up with Jenny and was shepherded out by the governess.

"Marshmallow," John chided the older man, poking the air with his fork. "You should have made her eat them herself."

"When you start eating liver and onions voluntarily, I'll make Bess eat eggs," Gil promised. "Want to come with us to the movies?" He named the picture they were going to see.

"Not me," John said pleasantly. "I'm going to Billings to see a man about some more acreage." He glanced at Kasie speculatively. "Want to tag along, Kasie?"

The question surprised her. While she was trying to think of a polite way to say she didn't, Gil answered for her.

"Kasie's going with us to the movies," he replied,

and his pale eyes dared her to argue. "The girls will have conniptions if we leave her behind. Besides, she likes cartoons. Don't you, Kasie?"

"I'm just crazy about them, Mr. Callister," she agreed with a tight smile, angry because he'd more or less forced her into agreeing to go.

"Mr. Callister was our father," Gil said firmly. "Don't use it with us."

She grimaced. "I work for you. It doesn't seem right."

John was gaping at her. "You're kidding."

"No, she isn't," Gil assured him. "When you have a free minute, get her to tell you why she braids her hair. It's a hoot."

She glared at Gil. "You cut that out."

He wiped his mouth with a white linen napkin and got to his feet. "I've got some phone calls to make before we go. We'll leave at one, Kasie."

"Phone calls on Sunday?" she asked John when his brother had left them alone.

"It's yesterday in some parts of the world, and tomorrow in some other parts," he reminded her. "You know how he is about business."

"Yes," she agreed.

"What amazes me," he mused, watching her, "is how much he grumbles about you. He loves women, as a rule. He's always doing little things to make the job easier for Mrs. Charters. He lets Pauline get away with only working three days of the week, when he needs a full-time secretary worse than I do. But he's hard on you."

52

"He doesn't like me," she said quietly. "He can't help it."

"You don't like him, either."

She smiled sheepishly. "I can't help it, either." She picked up on something he'd said earlier. "How can Pauline make ends meet with only a part-time job?" she asked curiously.

"She's independently wealthy," John told her. "She doesn't need a job at all, but she caught Gil at a weak moment. He doesn't have many of them, believe me. I think she attracted him at first. Now things have cooled and he's stuck with her. She's tenacious."

"Why would she need to work?" she wondered aloud.

"Because Gil needed a secretary, of course. She hasn't had any business training, and I don't doubt that the files are in a hellacious mess."

"Couldn't he get somebody else?"

"He tried to. Pauline cried all over him and he gave up."

"He doesn't look like a man who'd even notice tears," she said absently.

"Appearances are deceptive. You saw how he was when the dog threatened the girls," he reminded her. "He's not immune to tears."

"I'd need convincing," she said and grinned wickedly.

He leaned back in his chair with his coffee cup in his hand and studied her. "You're good with the kids," he said. "You must have spent a lot of time around children."

She lowered her eyes to her empty plate. "I did. I'm not formally taught or anything, but I do know a few things."

"It shows. I've never seen Bess respond to any of her various governesses. She liked you on sight."

"How many governesses has she had?" she asked curiously.

"Four. This year," he amended.

Her eyebrows arched. "Why so many?"

"Are you afraid of spiders, garter snakes, or frogs?" he asked.

She shook her head. "Why?"

"Well, the others were. They got downright twitchy about opening drawers or pulling down bedcovers," he recalled with a chuckle. "Bess likes garter snakes. She shared them with the governesses."

"Oh, dear," Kasie said.

"You see the point. That's why Miss Parsons was hired. She's the next best thing to a Marine DI, as you may have noticed."

Her face lightened. "So that's why he hired her. I did wonder."

John sighed. "I wish he'd hired her to do the tax work on the payroll instead. She's a natural, and since she's a retired accountant that experience would make her an asset. We have a firm of C.P.A.'s to do yearly stuff, but our bookkeeper who did payroll got married and moved to L.A. just before we hired you."

"And Miss Parsons got hired to look after the girls. She really dislikes children," she added.

"I know. But Gil refuses to believe it. He's been lax about work at the ranch for a while. He stayed on the road more and more, avoiding the memories after Darlene died. I felt bad for him, but things were going to pot here. I have to travel to show the bulls," he added, "because the more competitions we win, the higher the prices we can charge for stud fees or young bulls. The ranch can't run without anybody overseeing it." He pursed his lips as he studied her. "I gather that you said something to him about neglecting the girls. I thought so," he mused when she shifted uncomfortably. "I've told him, too, but he didn't listen to me. Apparently he listens to you."

"He's already tried to fire me once," she pointed out.

"You're still here," he replied.

"Yes. But I can't help but wonder for how much longer," she murmured, voicing her one real fear. "I could go back and live with my aunt, but it isn't fair to her. I have to work and support myself. This was the only full-time job that I was qualified for. Jobs are thin on the ground, regardless of the reports coming out about how great the economy is."

"How did you end up in Medicine Ridge in the first place?" he wondered.

"I was living with my aunt in Billings when I saw the ad for this job in the local paper. I'd already been all over Billings hoping for a full-time job and couldn't find one. This one seemed tailor-made for me."

"I'm glad you applied for it," he said. "There were

a lot of candidates, but we ruled out most of them in less than five minutes each. You were the only woman out there who could even type."

"You're kidding."

"No. They thought I wanted beauty instead of brains. I didn't." He smiled. "Not that you're bad on the eyes, Kasie. But I wasn't running a pageant."

"I was surprised that your brother hired me," she confessed. "He seemed to dislike me on sight. But when he found out how fast I could type, he was a lot less antagonistic."

He wasn't going to mention what Gil had said to him after he hired Kasie. It had been against Gil's better judgment, and he'd picked her appearance and her pert manner to pieces. It was interesting that Gil was antagonistic toward her. Very interesting.

"You're a whiz at the computer," John said. "A real asset. I didn't realize what you could do with a spreadsheet program until you modified ours. You're gifted."

"I love computers," she said with a smile. "Pauline is going to enjoy them, too, when she learns just a little more. Once she discovers the Internet, she'll be even more efficient. There are all sorts of Web sites dedicated to the cattle industry. It would be great for comparisons—even for buying and selling bulls. You could have your own Web site."

John let out a low whistle. "Funny, I hadn't even considered that. Kasie, it might revolutionize the way we do business, not to mention cutting down on the amount of travel we have to do every year."

"That's what I thought, too," she said, smiling at him.

"Mention it to Gil when you go to the movies," he coaxed. "Let's see what he thinks."

"He might like the idea better if it came from you," she said.

"I think he'll like it, period. I already do. Can you make a Web site?"

She grimaced. "No, I can't. But I know a woman who can," she added. "She works out of Billings. I met her when we were going to secretarial school. She's really good, and she doesn't charge an arm and a leg. I can get in touch with her, if you like."

"Go ahead. We do a lot of communication by e-mail, but neither of us even thought about putting cattle on our own site. It's a terrific idea!"

"You sound like Bess," Gil said from the doorway. "What's terrific?"

"We're going on the Internet," John said.

His big brother frowned. "The Internet?"

"Kasie can tell you what she's proposed. It could open new doors for us in marketing. It's international."

Gil was quick. He caught on almost at once. "You mean, get a Web site and use it to buy and sell cattle," he said.

"It will save you as much time as sending e-mail back and forth between potential buyers and sellers already does," she added.

"Good idea." Gil studied her with a curious smile. "Full of surprises aren't you, Miss Mayfield?"

"She's gifted," John said, grinning at his brother. "I told you so. Now maybe you can stop talking about firing her, hmm?"

Gil pressed his lips together and refused to rise to the bait. "It's almost one o'clock. If we're going to the movies, let's go. Kasie, fetch the girls."

She almost saluted, but he looked vaguely irritated. It looked as though nothing she suggested was ever going to please him. She wondered why she didn't just walk out and leave him to it. The thought was painful. She went up to get the little girls, more confused than ever.

Chapter 4

The girls chattered like birds all the way to town in Gil's black Jaguar. Kasie sat in front and listened patiently, smiling, while they told her all about the movie they were going to see. They'd seen the previews on television when they watched their Saturday morning cartoons.

It was a warm, pretty day, and trees and shrubs were blooming profusely. It should have been perfect, but Kasie was uneasy. Maybe she shouldn't have mentioned anything about Web sites, but it seemed an efficient way for Gil and John to move into Web-based commerce.

"You're brooding," Gil remarked. "Why?"

"I was wondering if I should have suggested anything about Internet business," she said.

"Why not? It's a good idea," he said, surprising her. "John told me about the Web site designer. Tomorrow, I want you to get in touch with her and get the process started."

"She'll need you to tell her what you want on the site."

"Okay."

She glanced in the back seat where the girls were sharing a book and enthusing over the pop-up sections.

"I brought it home for them yesterday," he commented, "and forgot to give it to them. They love books."

"That's the first step to getting them to love reading," she said, smiling at the little heads bowed over the books. "Reading to them at night keeps it going."

"Did your mother read to you?" he asked curiously.

"She probably did," she mused, smiling sadly. "But Kantor and I were very young when she and our father . . . died. Mama Luke read to us, when we were older."

"I suppose you liked science fiction," he murmured.

"How did you know?" she asked.

"You love computers," he said with a hint of a smile.

"I guess they do fit in with science fiction," she had to admit. She eyed him curiously. "What sort of books did you like to read?"

"Pirate stories, cowboy stories. Stuff like that. Now, it's genetics textbooks and management theory," he added wryly. "I hardly ever have time to read just for fun."

"Do your parents help you with the ranch?"

He seemed to turn to ice. "We don't talk about our parents," he said stiffly.

That sounded odd. But she was already in his bad book, so she didn't pursue it. "It's nice of you to take the girls to the movies."

He slowed for a turn, his expression taut. "I don't spend enough time with them," he said. "You were right about that. It isn't a lack of love. It's a lack of delegation. You'd be amazed how hard it is to find good managers who want to live on a cattle ranch."

"Maybe you don't advertise in a wide enough range," she suggested gently.

"What?"

She plunged ahead. "There are all sorts of trade magazines that carry ads with blind mailboxes," she said. "You can have replies sent to the newspaper and nobody has to know who you are."

"How do you know about the trade magazines?" he asked.

She grinned sheepishly. "I read them. Well, I ought to know something about cattle, since I work for a ranch, shouldn't I?"

He shook his head. "You really are full of surprises, Kasie."

"Kasie, what's this big word?" Bess asked, thrusting the book at her. Kasie took it and sounded the word out phonetically, coaching the little girl in its pronunciation. She took the book back and began to teach the word to Jenny.

"You're patient," Gil remarked. "I notice that Miss Parsons doesn't like taking time to teach them words."

"Miss Parsons likes numbers."

"Yes. She does." He pulled into the theater parking lot, which was full of parents and children. He got everyone out and locked the door, grimacing as they walked past several minivans.

"They're handy for little kids," Kasie said wickedly. "Mothers love them, I'm told."

"I love my kids, but I'm not driving a damned minivan," he muttered.

She grinned at his expression. The little girls ran to get in line, and struck up a conversation with a child they knew, whose bored mother perked up when she saw Gil approaching.

"Hi, Gil!" she called cheerily. "We're going to see the dinosaur movie! Is that why you're here?"

"That's the one," he replied, pulling bills out of his wallet. He gave one to each of the little girls, and they bought their own tickets. Gil bought his and Kasie's as they came to the window. "Hi, Amie," he called to the little girl with Bess and Jenny, and he smiled. She smiled back. She was as dark as his children were fair, with black eyes and hair like her mother's.

"We're going to sit with Amie, Daddy!" Bess said excitedly, waving her ticket and Jenny's.

"I guess that leaves me with you and . . . ?" the other woman paused deliberately.

"This is Kasie," Gil said, and took her unexpectedly by the arm, with a bland smile at Amie's mom. "You're welcome to join us, of course, Connie."

The other woman sighed. "No, I guess I'll sit with the girls. Nice to have seen you," she added, and moved ahead with the girls, looking bored all over again.

Gil slid his hand down into Kasie's. She reacted nervously to the unexpected touch, but his fingers clung, warm and strong against her own. He drew her along to the line already forming alongside the velvet ropes as the ticket takers prepared to let people through to the various theaters.

"Humor me," he said, and it looked as though he were whispering sweet nothings into her ear. "I'm the entrée, in case you haven't noticed."

Kasie glanced around and saw a number of women with little children and no man along, and two of them gave him deliberate, wistful glances and smiled.

"Single moms?" she whispered back, having to go on tiptoe.

He caught her around the waist and held her against his hip. "No. Get the picture?"

Her breath caught. "Oh, dear," she said heavily.

He looked down into her wide eyes. "You're such a child sometimes," he said softly. "You don't see ugliness, do you? You go through life looking for rainbows instead of rain."

"Habit," she murmured, fascinated by the pale blue lights in his eyes.

"It's a rather nice habit," he replied. The look lasted just a few seconds too long to be polite, and Kasie felt her heart begin to race. But then, the line shifted and diverted him. He moved closer to the ticket-taker, keeping the girls ahead carefully in sight while his arm drew Kasie along with him.

She liked the protectiveness of that muscular arm. He didn't look like a body-builder, all his movements were lithe and graceful. But he worked at physical labor from dawn until dusk most days. She'd seen him throw calves that had to be doctored. She'd seen him throw bulls, too. He was strong. Involuntarily she relaxed against him. It was delicious, the feeling of security it gave her to be close to him, to the warm strength of him.

The soft movement caught him off guard and sent a jolt of sensation through him that he hadn't felt in a long time. He looked down at her with curious, turbulent eyes that she didn't see. She was smiling and waving at the girls, who were darting off down into the theater with the little girl and her mother.

"They like you," he said.

"I like them."

He handed their tickets to the uniformed girl, who smiled as she handed back the stubs and pointed the way to the theater that was showing the cartoon movie.

Gil caught Kasie's hand in his and drew her lazily along with him through the crowd of children and parents until they reached the theater. But instead of going down to the front, he drew Kasie to an isolated double-seat in the very back row and sat down beside her. His arm went over the back of the chair as the theater darkened and the previews began showing.

Kasie was electrified by the shift in their relationship. She felt his lean fingers on her shoulder, bringing her closer, and his cheek rested against her temple. She hadn't ever been to a movie with a man. There had been a blind double date once, and the boy sat on his own side of the seat and looked nervous until they got home again. This was worlds away from that experience.

"Comfortable?" he asked at her ear, and his voice was like velvet.

"Yes," she said unsteadily.

His chest rose and fell and he found himself paying a lot more attention to the feel of Kasie's soft hair against his skin than the movie. She smelled of spring roses. Her hair was soft, and had a faint herbal scent of its own. Twenty-two. She was twenty-two. He was thirty-two, and she'd already said that he was too old for her.

He scowled as he thought about that difference. She needed someone as young as she was, with that same vulnerable, kind, generous spirit. He had two little girls and a high-pressure business that gave him little free time. He was still grieving, in a way, for Darlene, whom he'd loved since grammar school. But there was something about Kasie that made him hungry. It wasn't desire, although he was aware of heady sensations when she was close to him. No, it was the sort of hunger a man got when he was standing outside in the snow with a wet coat and soaked jeans, looking through the window at a warm, glowing fireplace. He couldn't really explain the feelings. They made him uneasy.

He noticed that she was still a little stiff. He touched

a curl at her ear. "Hey," he whispered.

She turned her head and looked up at him in the semidarkness.

"I'm not hitting on you," he whispered into her ear. "Okay?"

She relaxed. "Okay."

The obvious relief in her voice made him feel guilty and offended. He moved his arm back to the chair and forced himself to watch the movie. He had to remember that Kasie worked for him. It wasn't fair to use her to ward off other women. But . . . was it really that?

The dinosaur movie was really well-done, Kasie thought as she became involved in the storyline and the wonder of creatures that looked really alive up there on the screen. It was a bittersweet sort of cartoon, though, and she was sorry for the little girls. Because when it was over, Bess and Jenny came to them crying about the dinosaurs that had died in the film.

"Oh, sweetheart, it was only a movie," Kasie said at once, and bent to pick up Bess, hugging her close. "Just a movie. Okay?"

"But it was so sad, Kasie," cried the little girl. "Why do things have to die?"

"I don't know, baby," she said softly, and her eyes closed for an instant on a wave of remembered pain. She'd lost so many people she loved.

Gil had Jenny up in his arms, and they walked out of the theater carrying the children. Behind them, other mothers were trying to explain about extinction.

"There, there, baby," he cooed at Jenny and kissed her wet eyes. "It was only make-believe. Dinosaurs don't really talk, you know, and they had brains the size of peas." He shifted her and smiled. "Hey, remember what I told you about chickens, about how they'll walk right up to a rattlesnake and let it strike them? Well, dinosaurs didn't even have brains that big."

"They didn't?" Bess asked from her secure hold on Kasie.

"They didn't," Gil said. "If a meteor had struck them, they'd be standing right in its path waiting for it. And they wouldn't be discussing it, either."

Kasie laughed as she looked at Gil, delighted at the way he handled the sticky situation. He was, she thought, a marvelous parent.

"Can we get some ice cream on the way home?" Bess asked then, wiping her tears.

"You bet. We'll stop by the yogurt place."

"Thanks, Daddy!" Bess cried.

"You're the nicest daddy," Jenny murmured against his throat.

"You really are, you know," Kasie agreed as they strapped the little girls into the back seat.

His eyes met hers across the children. "I'm a veteran daddy," he told her dryly.

"Is that what it is?" Kasie chuckled.

"You get better with practice, or so they tell me. Do you like frozen yogurt? I get them that instead of ice cream. It's healthy stuff."

"I like it, too," Kasie said as she got into the front seat beside him.

"We'll get some to take home for Mrs. Charters and Miss Parsons," he added, "so that we don't get blamed for ruining their appetites for supper."

"Now that's superior thinking," Kasie had to admit.

He started the engine and eased them out of the crowded parking lot.

The yogurt shop was a few miles from home. They stopped and got the treat in carryout cups, because Gil was expecting a phone call from a buyer out of state.

"I don't like to work on Sundays," he remarked as they drove home. "But sometimes it's unavoidable."

"Do you ever take the girls to church?"

He hesitated. "Well . . . no."

She was watching him with those big, soft gray eyes, in which there wasn't condemnation or censure. It was almost as if she knew that his faith had suffered since the death of his wife. No, for longer than that. It had suffered since childhood, when his parents had . . .

"I haven't gone for several months, myself," Kasie remarked quietly. She twisted her purse slowly in her hands. "If I . . . start back, I could take them with me, if you didn't mind."

"I don't mind," he replied.

Her eyes softened and she smiled at him.

He tore his gaze away from that warm affection and forced it back to the road. His hand tightened on the steering wheel. She really was getting to him. He wished he knew some way to head off trouble. He found her far too attractive, and she continued to make her lack of receptiveness known. He didn't want to do something stupid and send her looking for another job.

"I enjoyed today," he said after a minute. "But you remember that Miss Parsons is supposed to be responsible for the girls," he added with a stern glance. "You have enough to do keeping John's paperwork current. Understand?"

"Yes, I do. I'll try very hard to stop interfering," she promised.

"Good. Pauline is out of town for the next week, but she'll be home in time for the pool party we're giving next Saturday. She'll be in the office the following Monday morning. You can give her another computer lesson."

She grimaced. "She doesn't like me."

"I know. Don't let it worry you. She's efficient."

She wasn't, but apparently she'd managed to conceal it from Gil. Kasie wondered how he'd managed not to notice the work Pauline didn't do.

"Did John have a secretary before me?" she asked suddenly.

"He did, and she was a terrific one, too. But she quit with only a week's notice."

"Did she say why?" she fished with apparent unconcern.

"Something about being worked to death. John didn't buy it. She didn't have that much to do."

She did, if she was doing John's work and having

Gil's pawned off on her as well. Kasie's eyes narrowed. Well, she wasn't going to get away with it now. If Pauline started expecting Kasie to do her job for her, she was in for a surprise.

"Funny," Gil murmured as he turned onto the black shale ranch road that led to the Double C. "Pauline said she couldn't use the computer, but she always had my herd records printed out. Even if they weren't updated properly."

Kasie didn't say a word. Surely he'd work it out by himself one day. She glanced back at the girls, who were still contentedly eating frozen yogurt out of little cups. They were so pretty and sweet. Her heart ached just looking at them. Sandy had been just Bess's age . . .

She bit down hard on her lip. She mustn't cry. Tears were no help at all. She had to look ahead, not backward.

Gil pulled up in front of the house and helped Kasie get the girls out.

"Thanks for the movie," Kasie told him, feeling shy now.

"My pleasure," he said carelessly. "Come on, girls, let's get you settled with Miss Parsons. Daddy's got to play rancher for a while."

"Can't we play, too?" Bess asked, clinging to his hand.

"Sure," he said. "Just as soon as you can compare birth weight ratios and compute projected weaning weight."

Bess made a face. "Oh, Daddy!"

"I'll make a rancher out of you one day, young lady," he said with a grin.

"Billy's dad said he was sure glad he had a son instead of girls. Daddy, do you ever wish me and Jenny was boys?" she asked.

He stopped, dropped to one knee and hugged the child close. "Daddy loves little girls," he said softly. "And he wouldn't trade you and Jenny for all the boys in the world. You tell Billy I said that."

Bess chuckled. "I will!" She kissed his cheek with a big smack. "I love you, Daddy!"

"I love you, too, little chick."

Jenny, jealous, had to have a hug, too, and they ended up each clinging to a strong, lean hand as they went into the house.

Kasie watched them, feeling more lost and alone than she had in months. She ached to be part of a family again. Watching Gil with the girls only emphasized what she'd lost.

She went up onto the porch and up the staircase slowly, her hand smoothing over the silky wood of the banister as she tried once again to come to grips with her loss.

She was curled up in her easy chair watching an old movie on television when there was a soft knock at the door just before it opened. Bess and Jenny sneaked in wearing their gowns and bathrobes and slippers, peering cautiously down the hall before they closed the door.

"Hello," Kasie said with a smile, opening her arms

as they clambered up into the big chair with her and cuddled close. "You smell nice."

"We had baths," Bess said. "Miss Parsons said we was covered with chocolate sauce." She giggled. "We splashed her."

"You bad babies," she chided softly and kissed little cheeks.

"Could you tell us a story?" they asked.

"Sure. What would you like to hear?"

"The one with the bears."

"Okay." She started the story, speaking in all the different parts, while they snuggled close and listened with attention.

Just to see if they were really listening, she added, "And then the wolf huffed and puffed . . ."

"No, Kasie!" Bess interrupted. "That's the pig story!"

"Is it?" she exclaimed. "All right, then. Well, the bears came home . . ."

"Huffing and puffing?" came a deep, amused query from the doorway. The little girls glanced at him, looking guilty and worried. "Miss Parsons is looking for you two fugitives," he drawled. "If I were you, I'd get into my beds real fast. She's glowering."

"Goodness! We got to go, Kasie!" Bess said, and she and Jenny scrambled to their feet and ran past their father down the hall, calling good-nights as they went.

Gil studied Kasie from the doorway. She was wearing her own white gown, with a matching cotton robe this time, and her long hair waved around her

71

shoulders. She looked very young.

"You weren't reading from a book. What did you do, memorize the story?" he asked curiously.

"I guess so," she confided, smiling. "I've told it so many times, I suppose I do have it down pretty well."

"Who did you tell it to?" he asked reasonably.

The smile never faded, but she withdrew behind it. "A little girl who stayed with us sometimes," she replied.

"I see."

"They came in and asked for a story," she explained. "I hated telling them to go away . . ."

"I haven't said a word."

"You did," she reminded him worriedly. "I know that Miss Parsons looks after them. I'm not trying to interfere."

"I know that. But it's making things hard for her when they come to you instead," he said firmly.

She grimaced. "I can't hurt their feelings."

"I'll speak to them." He held up a hand when she started to protest. "I'll speak to them nicely," he added. "I won't make an issue of it."

She hesitated. "Okay."

"You have your own duties," he continued. "It isn't fair to let you take on two jobs, no matter how you feel about it. I don't pay Miss Parsons to sit and read tax manuals."

Her eyes widened. "You're kidding," she said, sitting up straight. "She reads tax manuals? What for? Did you ask her?"

"I did. She says she reads them for pleasure," he

72

said. "Apparently she didn't really want to retire from the accounting business, but she was faced with a clerical position or retirement," he added with a droll smile.

"Oh, dear."

He pushed away from the door facing. "Don't stay up too late. John needs to get an early start. He'll be away for a week showing Ebony King on the road."

"He's the new young bull," Kasie recalled. "He eats corn out of my hand," she added with a smile. "I never thought of bulls as being gentle."

"They're a real liability if they're not," he pointed out. "A bull that size could trample a man with very little difficulty."

"I guess he could." She stood up, with her hands in the pockets of the cotton robe. "I'm sorry about the girls coming in here."

"Oh, hell, I don't mind," he said on a rough breath. "But it isn't wise to let them get too attached to you, Kasie. You know it, and you know why."

"They think you're going to marry Pauline," she blurted out, and then flushed at having been so personal with him.

"I haven't thought a lot about remarrying," he replied quietly. His eyes went over her with a suddenly intent appraisal. "But maybe I should. They're getting to the age where they're going to need a woman's hand in their lives. I love them, but I can't see things from a female point of view."

"You've done marvelously with them so far," she

told him. "They're polite and generous and loving."

"So was their mother," he remarked and for a few seconds, his face was lined with grief before he got it under control. "She loved them."

"You said Bess was like her," she reminded him.

"Yes," he said at once. "She had long, wavy blond hair, just that same color. Jenny looks more like me. But Bess is more like me."

She smiled. "I've noticed. She has a very hard head when she doesn't want to do something."

He shrugged. "Being stubborn isn't always a bad thing. Persistence is the key to most successes in life."

"Yes." She searched his hard face, seeing the years of work and worry. It was a good, strong face, but it wasn't handsome.

He was looking at her, too, and something stirred inside him, a need that he had to work to put down. He moved out the door. "Sleep well, Kasie," he said curtly.

"You, too."

He closed the door behind him, without looking at her again. She went back to her movie, but with much less enthusiasm.

Chapter 5

The week went by slowly, and the girls, to Kasie's dismay, became her shadows. She worried herself sick trying to keep Gil from noticing, especially after the harsh comments he'd made about her job responsibilities. It didn't help that she kept remembering the feel of his arm around her at the movie theater, and the warm clasp of his big lean hand in her own. She was afraid to even look at him, because she was afraid her attraction to him might show.

Saturday came and the house was full of strangers. Kasie found it hard to mix with high society people, so she stuck to Miss Parsons and the girls. Miss Parsons took the opportunity to sneak back inside the house while Kasie watched the girls. Everything went well at first, because Gil was too busy with guests to notice that Miss Parsons was missing. But not for long. Kasie had given the girls a beach ball to play with, which was her one big mistake of the morning.

It wouldn't have been so bad if she'd just let the children's beach ball fly into the swimming pool in the first place. The problem was that, if she didn't stop it, Pauline was going to get it in the mouth, which wouldn't improve the already-bad situation between her and Kasie. Bess and Jenny didn't like Gil Callister's secretary. Neither did Kasie, but she loved the little girls and didn't want them to get into trouble. So she gave in to an impulse, and tried valiantly to divert the ball from its unexpecting target.

Predictably, she overreached, lost her footing and made an enormous splash as she landed, fully clothed, in the deep end. And, of course, she couldn't swim . . .

Gil looked up from the prospectus he'd been reading when he heard the splash. He connected Kasie's fall, the beach ball, and his two little blond giggling daughters at once. He shook his head and grimaced. He put aside the prospectus and dived in to save Kasie, Bermuda shorts, Hawaiian shirt and all.

Her late parents had lived long enough to see the irony of the second name they'd given her. Her middle name was Grace, but she wasn't graceful. She was all long legs and arms. She wasn't pretty, but she had a lovely body, and the thin white dress she was wearing became transparent in the water. It was easily noticed that she was wearing only the flimsiest of briefs and a bra that barely covered her pert breasts. Just the thing, she thought miserably, to wear in front of the Callisters' business partners who were here for a pool party on the big ranch. Feline blond Pauline Raines was laughing her head off at Kasie's desperate treading of water. Just you wait, lady, she fumed. Next time I'll give Bess a soccer ball to bean you with and I won't step in the way . . . !

Her head went under as her arms gave out. She took a huge breath as powerful arms encircled and lifted her clear of the deep water. It would have to be Gil who rescued her, she thought miserably. John wasn't even looking their way. He'd have dived in after her in a minute, she knew, if he'd seen her fall. But while he was nice, and kind, he wasn't Gil, who was beginning to have a frightening effect on Kasie's heart. She glanced at Pauline as she spluttered. Kasie wished that she was beautiful like Pauline. She looked the very image of an efficient secretary. Kasie had great typing speed, dictation skills and organizational expertise, but she was only ordinary-looking. Besides, she was a social disaster, and she'd just proved it to Gil and all the guests.

Gil had been unexpectedly kind to her at the theater when he'd taken her with the girls to see the movie. She still tingled, remembering his hand holding hers. This, however, was much worse. Her breasts were almost bare in the thin blouse, and she felt the hard muscular wall of his chest with wonder and pleasure and a little fear, because she'd never felt such heady sensations in her body before. She wondered if he'd fire her for making a scene at this pool party, to which a lot of very wealthy and prominent cattlemen and their wives had been invited.

To give him credit, she hadn't exactly inspired confidence on the job in the past few weeks. Two weeks earlier, she tripped on the front steps and landed in a rosebush at the very feet of a visiting cattleman from Texas who'd almost turned purple trying not to laugh. Then there had been the ice-cream incident last week, which still embarrassed her. Bess had threatened Kasie with a big glop of chocolate ice cream. While Kasie was backing away, laughing helplessly, Gil had come into the house in dirty chaps and boots and shirt with his hat jerked low over one blue eye and his mouth a thin line, with blood streaming from a cut on his forehead. Bess had thrown the ice cream at Kasie, who ducked, just in time for it to hit Gil right in the forehead. While he was wiping it off, Kasie grabbed the spoon from Bess and waited for the explosion as her boss wiped the ice cream away and looked at her. Those blue eyes could cut like diamonds. They actually glittered. But he hadn't said a word. He'd just looked at her, before he turned and continued down the hall to the staircase that led up to his room.

Now, here she was half-drowned from a swimming pool accident, having made a spectacle of herself yet again.

"I wonder if I could get work in Hollywood?" she sputtered as she hung on for dear life. "There must be a market for terminal clumsiness somewhere!"

Gil raised an eyebrow and gave her a slow, speaking glance before he pulled her close against his chest and turned toward the concrete steps at the far end. He walked up out of the pool, streaming water, and started toward the house. "Don't struggle, Kasie," he said at her temple, and his voice sounded odd.

"Sorry," she coughed. "You can put me down, now. I'm okay. I can walk."

"If I put you down, you're going to become the entertainment," he said enigmatically at her ear. He looked over his shoulder. "John, look after the girls

78

until I get back!" he called.

"Oh, I'll watch them, Gil!" Pauline interrupted lazily. "Come over here, girls!" she called, without even looking in their direction.

"John will watch them," Gil said emphatically and didn't move until his lean, lanky brother jumped up and went toward his nieces, grinning.

Gil went up the staircase with Kasie held close to his chest. "Why can't you swim?" he asked.

His deep, slow voice made her feel funny. So did the close, almost intimate contact with him. She nibbled on her lower lip, feeling soggy and disheveled and embarrassed. "I'm afraid of the water."

"Why?" he persisted.

She wouldn't answer him. It would do no good, and she didn't want to remember. Probably he'd never seen anyone drown. "Sorry I messed up the pool party," she murmured.

He shook her gently as they passed the landing and paused at her bedroom door. "Stop apologizing every second word," he said curtly as he put her down. He held her there with two big, lean hands on her upper arms and studied her intently in the dim light of the wall sconces.

The feel of all that warm strength against her made her giddy. She'd never been so close to him before. He was ten years older than Kasie, and he had an authority and maturity that must have been apparent even when he'd been her age. She had tried to think of him as Bess and Jenny's daddy, but after their closeness at the movie theater, it was almost impossible to think of him as anything but a mature, sexy man.

"I can't seem to make you understand that the girls are Miss Parsons' responsibility, not yours!" He saw her faint flush and scowled down at her. "Speaking of Miss Parsons, where in hell is she?"

She cleared her throat and pushed back a soggy strand of dark hair. "She's in the office."

"Doing what?"

She shifted, but he didn't let go of her arms. That unblinking, ferocious blue stare robbed her of a smart retort. "All right," she said heavily. "She's doing the withholding on John's tax readout." He didn't speak. She looked up and grimaced. "Well, I'm not up on tax law, and she is."

"So you traded duties without permission, is that it?"

She hesitated. "Yes. I'm sorry. But it's just for today! You already know that she doesn't . . . well, she doesn't like children very much, really, and I hate taxes . . ."

"I know."

"I shouldn't have given them the beach ball. I thought they were going into the shallow part of the pool with it. And then Bess threw it . . ."

"Right at Pauline's expensive new coiffure," Gil finished for her. He pursed his sensuous lips and searched her face. "You won't tell on them, of course. You took the blame for the ice cream, too. And when one of Jenny's toys tripped you on the front steps and you went into the rosebush, you

80

blamed that on clumsiness."

"You knew?" she asked, surprised.

"I've been a father for five years," he mused. "I know all sorts of things." His pale blue eyes slid very slowly down Kasie's wet dress and narrowed on what was showing. She had the most delicious body. Every line and curve of it was on view where the thin dress was plastered to her body. Her breasts were perfectly shaped and the nipples were dusky. The feel of her against his chest, even through her wet blouse and his cotton shirt, had almost knocked the breath out of him. It upset him that he was noticing these things about her. He was beginning to react to them, too. He had to get out of here. She was so young . . .

He cursed under his breath. "You'd better change," he said curtly. He turned on his heel and went toward the staircase.

"About Miss Parsons . . . !" she called after him, in one last attempt to ward off retribution.

"You might as well consider the girls your job from now on," he said angrily. "I can see that it's a losing battle to keep you away from them. I'll give Miss Parsons to John. He won't enjoy the view as much, but keeping out of prison because we can't figure out tax forms might sweeten the deal," he said, without breaking stride. "When you have some spare time, you can continue giving Pauline computer lessons. That includes Monday morning. Mrs. Charters can watch the girls while you work with Pauline."

"But I'm not a trained governess. I'm a secretary!" she insisted.

"Great. You can let Bess dictate letters to you for her dolls."

"But . . . !"

It was too late. He never argued. He just kept walking. She threw up her hands and went back into her room. She started toward the bathroom to change out of her wet things when she got a look at herself in the mirror. The whole outfit was transparent. She remembered Gil's intent stare and blushed all the way to her toes. No wonder he'd been looking at her. Everything she had was on view! She wondered how she'd ever be able to look him in the eye again.

She changed and went back to the pool party, dejected and miserable. It was hard to believe that she'd not even had a mild crush on John when she first went to work for the Callisters. He was handsome, and very sexy, but she just didn't feel that way about him. Fortunately he'd never felt that way about her, either. John had some secret woman in his past, and now he didn't get serious about anyone. Kasie had heard that from Mrs. Charters, who was a veritable storehouse of information about it. John didn't look to Kasie like a man with a broken heart. But maybe he played the field to camouflage it.

Kasie had never really been in love. She'd had crushes on TV celebrities and movie stars, and on boys at school—and one summer she'd had a real case on a boy who lived near Mama Luke, her aunt, in Billings. But those had all been very innocent, limited to kisses and light caresses and not much desire.

All that had changed when Gil Callister held her hand at the movies. And when Gil had carried her up the staircase this morning, she was on fire with pleasure. She was still shivery with new sensations, which she didn't understand at all. Gil was her boss and he disliked her. She'd been spending more time with the girls than the grown-ups because John didn't like to do paperwork and he was always dodging dictation. He could usually be found out with the men on the ranch, helping with whatever routine task was going on at the time. Gil did that, too, of course, but not because he didn't like paperwork. Gil rarely ever sat still.

Mrs. Charters said it was because he'd loved his wife and had never gotten over her unexpected death from a freak horseback-riding accident. She was only twenty-six years old.

That had been only three years ago. Since then, Gil had hired a succession of nurses, at first, and then motherly governesses to watch over the girls. Old Mrs. Harris had retired and then Gil had hired Miss Parsons in desperation, over a virtual flood of young marriageable women who had their eye on either Gil or John. Kasie remembered Gil saying that he had no interest in marriage ever again. At that time, she couldn't have imagined feeling attracted to a widowed man with two children who had the personality of a spitting cobra.

For her first few weeks on the job, he'd watched Kasie. He hadn't wanted his children around Kasie, and made it plain. Amazing, how much that had hurt.

They were such darling little girls.

At least, she thought, now she could spend tim with them and not have to sneak around doing it. G might not like her, but he couldn't deny that h daughters did. Probably he felt that he didn't have choice.

Kasie was going to miss the secretarial work, an she wondered how Gil would manage with Paulin who absolutely hated clerical duties. The woman onl did it to be near Gil, but he didn't seem to realize i Or if he did, he didn't care.

She tried to picture Gil married to Pauline and wounded her. Pauline was shallow and selfish. Sh didn't really like the girls, and she'd probably fin some way to get them out of her hair when she and G married, if they did. Kasie hated the very idea of suc a marriage, but she was a little nobody in the worl and Gil Callister was a millionaire. She couldn't eve tease him or flirt with him, because he might think sh was after him for his wealth. It made her sel conscious, so she became uneasy around him ar tongue-tied to boot.

That made him even more irritable. Sunday afte noon there was another storm and he and the men h; to go out and work the cattle. He came in just aft dark, drenched, unfastening his shirt on the way int the office. His hair was plastered to his scalp and h spurs jingled as he walked, his leather bat-wing chaj making flapping noises with every stride of his lon powerful jean-clad legs. His boots were soaked, to and caked with mud.

"Mrs. Charters will be after you," Kasie remarked as she lifted her eyes from the badly scribbled notes John had left, which Miss Parsons had asked her to help decipher. Miss Parsons had already gone up to bed, anticipating a very early start on work the next morning.

"It's my damned house," he shot at her irritably, running a hand through his drenched hair to get it off his forehead. "I can drip wherever I please!"

"Suit yourself," Kasie replied. "But red mud won't come out of Persian wool carpets."

He gave her a hard glare, but he sat down in a chair and pulled off the mud-caked boots, tossing them onto the wide brick hearth of the fireplace, where they wouldn't soil anything delicate. His white socks were soaked as well, but he didn't take them off. He sat down behind his desk, picked up the telephone and made a call.

"Where are the girls?" he asked while he waited for the call to be answered.

"Watching the new *Pokémon* movie up in their room," Kasie said. "Miss Parsons can't read John's handwriting, so I'm deciphering this for her so she can start early tomorrow morning on the payroll and the quarterly estimated taxes that are due in June. If that's all right," she added politely.

He just glared at her. "Hello, Lonnie?" he said suddenly into the telephone receiver he was holding. "Can you give me the name of that mechanic who worked on Harris's truck last month? Yes, the one who doesn't need a damned computer to tell him what's wrong with the engine. Got his number? Just a minute." He fished in the drawer for a pen, grabbed an envelope and wrote a number on it. "Sure thing. Thanks." He hung up and dialed again.

While he spoke to the mechanic, Kasie finished transcribing John's terrible handwriting neatly for Miss Parsons.

Gil hung up and got to his feet, retrieving his boots. "If you've got a few minutes free, I need you to take some dictation for me," he told Kasie.

"I'll be glad to."

He gave her a narrow appraisal. "I've got a man coming over to look at my cattle truck," he added. "If he gets here while I'm in the shower, show him into the living room and don't let him leave. He can listen to an engine and tell you what's wrong with it."

"But it's Sunday," she began.

"I need the truck to haul cattle tomorrow. I'm sure he went to church this morning, so it's all right," he assured her dryly. "Besides . . ."

The ringing of the phone interrupted him. He jerked up the receiver. "Callister," he said.

There was a pause, during which his face became harder than Kasie had ever seen it. "Yes," he replied to a question. "I'll talk to John when he gets back in, but I can tell you what the answer will be." He smiled coldly. "I'm sure that if you use your imagination, you can figure that out without too much difficulty. No, I don't. I don't give a damn. Do what you please with them." There was a longer pause and Kasie thought she'd never seen such coldness in a man's eyes. "I

86

don't need a thing, thanks. Yes. You do that."

He hung up. "My parents," he said harshly. "With an invitation to come and bring the girls to their estate on Long Island next week."

"Are you going?"

He looked briefly sardonic. "They're hosting a party for some people who are interested in seeing what a real cattleman looks like," he said surprisingly. "They're trying to sell them on an advertising contract for their sports magazine and they think John and I might be useful." He sounded bitter and angry. "They try this occasionally, but John and I don't go. They can make money on their own. I'll be upstairs if the mechanic comes. Tell him the truck's in the barn with one of my men. He can go right on out."

"Okay."

He walked out and Kasie stared after him. The conversation with his parents hadn't been pleasant for him. He seemed to dislike them intensely. She knew that they were never mentioned around the girls, and John never spoke of them, either. She wondered what they'd done to make their sons so hostile. Then she remembered what Gil had said, about their being used by their parents only to make money, and it all began to make sense. Perhaps they didn't really want children at all. What a pity, that their sons were nothing more than sales incentives to them.

The mechanic did come while Gil was upstairs. Kasie went with him onto the long porch and showed him where the barn was, so that he could drive on down there and park his truck. The rain had stopped, though, so he didn't have to worry about getting wet. There was a pleasant dripping sound off the eaves of the house, and the delicious smell of wet flowers in the darkness.

Kasie sat down in the porch swing and rocked it into motion. It was a perfect night, now that the storm had abated. She could hear crickets, or maybe frogs, chirping all around the flowering shrubs that surrounded the front porch. It reminded her, for some reason, of Africa. She vaguely remembered sitting in a porch swing with her mother and Kantor when their father was away working. There were the delicious smells of cooking from the house, and the spicy smells drifting from the harbor nearby, as well as the familiar sound of African workers singing and humming as they worked around the settlement. It was a long time ago, when she still had a family. Now, except for Mama Luke, she was completely alone. It was a cold, empty feeling.

The screen door suddenly opened and Gil came out onto the porch. His blond hair was still damp, faintly unruly at the edges and tending to curl. He was wearing a blue checked Western shirt with clean jeans and nice boots. He looked just the way a working cowboy should when he was cleaned up, she thought, trying to imagine him a century earlier.

"Is the mechanic here?" he asked abruptly when he spotted Kasie in the swing.

"Yes, I sent him on down to the barn."

He went down the steps gracefully and stalked to the barn. He was gone about five minutes and when he came out of the barn, so did the mechanic. They shook hands and the mechanic drove off.

"A fuse," he murmured, shaking his head as he came up the steps and dropped into the swing at Kasie's side. "A damned fuse, and the whole panel went down. Imagine that."

"Sometimes it's the little things that give the most trouble," she murmured, shy with him.

He put an arm behind her and rocked the swing into motion. "I like the way you smell, Kasie," he said lazily. "You always remind me of roses."

"I'm allergic to perfume," she confided. "The florals are the only ones I can wear without sneezing my head off."

"Where are my babies?" he asked.

"Mrs. Charters is baking cookies with them in the kitchen," she said, smiling. "They love to cook. So do I. We've all learned a lot from Mrs. Charters."

He looked down at her in the darkness. One lean hand went to the braid at the back of her head, and he tugged on it gently. "You're mysterious," he murmured. "I don't really know anything about you."

"There's not much to tell," she told him. "I'm just ordinary."

He shifted, and she felt his powerful thigh against her leg. Her body came alive with fleeting little stabs of pleasure. She could feel her breath catching in her throat as she breathed. He was too close.

She started to move, but it was too late. His arm curled her into his body, and the warm, hard pressure of his mouth pushed her head back against the swing while he fed hungrily on her lips.

Part of her wanted to resist, but a stronger part was completely powerless. She reached up and put her arms around his neck and opened her lips for him. She felt him stiffen, hesitate, catch his breath. Then his mouth became rough and demanding, and he dragged her across his legs, folding her close while he kissed her until her mouth was swollen and tender.

He nibbled her upper lip, fighting to breathe normally. "Don't let me do this," he warned.

"You're bigger than I am," she murmured breathlessly.

"That's no excuse at all."

Her fingers trailed over his hard mouth and down to his chest where they rested. She stared at the wide curve of his mouth with a kind of wonder that a man like this, good-looking and charming and wealthy, would look twice at a chestnut mouse like Kasie. Perhaps he needed glasses.

He touched her oval face, tracing its soft lines in a warm, damp darkness that was suddenly like an exotic, faraway place. Kasie felt as if she'd come home. Impulsively, she let her head slide down his arm until it rested in the crook of his elbow. She watched his expression harden, heard his breathing change. His lean fingers moved down her chin and throat until they were at the top button of her shirt-waist dress. They hesitated there.

She lay looking up at him patiently, curiously, ablaze with unfamiliar longings and delight.

"Kasie," he whispered, and his long fingers began to

sensually move the top button out of its buttonhole. As it came free, he heard her soft gasp, felt the jerk of her body, and knew that this was new territory for her.

His hand started to slide gently into the opening he'd made. He watched Kasie, lying so sweetly in his embrace, giving him free license with her innocence, and he shivered with desire.

But even as he felt the soft warmth of the skin at her collarbone, laughing young voices came drifting out onto the porch as the front door opened.

Gil moved Kasie back into her own seat abruptly and stood up.

"Daddy's home!" Bess cried, and she and Jenny ran to him, to be scooped up and kissed heartily.

"I'll, uh, just go and get my pad so that you can dictate that letter you mentioned," Kasie said as she got up, too.

"You will not," Gil said, his voice still a little husky. "Go to bed, Kasie. It can wait. In the morning, you can tutor Pauline on the computer, so that she can take over inputting the cattle records. John won't be in until late tonight, and he leaves early tomorrow for the cattle show in San Antonio. There's nothing in the office that can't wait."

She was both disappointed and relieved. It was getting harder to deny Gil anything he wanted. She couldn't have imagined that she was such a wanton person only a few weeks ago. She didn't know what to do.

"Okay, I'll call it a night," she said, trying to disguise her nervousness. "Good night, babies," she told

Bess and Jenny with a smile. "Sleep tight."

"Will you tell us a story, Kasie?" Bess began.

"I'll tell you a story tonight. Kasie needs her rest. All right?" he asked the girls.

"All right, Daddy," Jenny murmured, laying her sleepy head on his shoulder.

They all went upstairs together. Kasie didn't quite meet his eyes as she went down the hall to her own room. She didn't sleep very much, either.

Chapter 6

Pauline Raines was half an hour late Monday morning. Gil had already gone out to check on some cattle that was being shipped off. John had left before daylight to fly to San Antonio, where the cattle trailer was taking his champion bull, Ebony King, for the cattle show. While the girls took their nap, Kasie helped Miss Parsons with John's correspondence and fielded the telephone. Now that it was just past roundup, things weren't quite as hectic, but sales reports were coming in on the culled cattle being shipped, and they weren't even all on the computer yet. Neither were most of the new calf crop.

Miss Parsons had gone to the post office when Pauline arrived wearing a neat black suit with a fetching blue scarf. She glared at Kasie as she threw her purse down on the chair.

"Here I am," she said irritably. "I don't usually come in before ten, but Gil said I had to be early, to work on this stupid computer. I don't see why I need to learn it."

"Because you'll have to put in all the information we're getting about the new calves and replacement heifers," Kasie explained patiently. "It's backing up."

"You can do that," Pauline said haughtily. "You're John's secretary."

"Not anymore," she replied calmly. "I'm going to take care of the girls while Miss Parsons takes my place in John's office. She's going to handle all the tax work."

That piece of information didn't please Pauline. "You're a secretary," she pointed out.

"That's what I told Mr. Callister, but it didn't change his mind," Kasie replied tersely.

"So now I'll have to do all your work while Miss Parsons does taxes? I won't! Surely you'll have enough free time to put these records on the computer! Two little girls don't require much watching. Just put them in front of the television!"

Kasie almost bit her tongue right through keeping back a hot reply. "It isn't going to be hard to use the computer. It will save you hours of paperwork."

Pauline gave her a glare. "Debbie always put these things on the computer."

"Debbie quit because she couldn't do two jobs at once," Kasie said, and was vindicated for the jibe when she saw Pauline's discomfort. "You really will enjoy the time the computer saves you, once you understand how it works."

"I don't need this job, didn't anyone tell you?" the

93

older woman asked. "I'm wealthy. I only do it to be near Gil. It gives us more time together, while we're seeing how compatible we are. Which reminds me, don't think you're onto a cushy job looking after those children," she added haughtily. "Gil and I are going to be looking for a boarding school very soon."

"Boarding school?" Kasie exclaimed, horrified.

"I've already checked out several," Pauline said. "It isn't good for little girls to become too attached to their fathers. It interferes with Gil's social life."

"I hadn't noticed."

Pauline frowned. "What do you mean, you hadn't noticed?"

"Well, Mr. Callister is almost a generation older than I am," she said deliberately.

"Oh." Pauline smiled secretively. "I see."

"He's a very kind man," Kasie emphasized, "but I don't think of him in that way," she added, lying through her teeth.

Pauline for once seemed speechless.

"Here, let's get started," Kasie said as she turned on the computer, trying to head off trouble. She hoped that comment would keep her out of trouble with Pauline, who obviously considered Gil Callister her personal property. Kasie had enough problems without adding a jealous secretary to them. Even if she did privately think Gil was the sexiest man she'd ever known.

Pauline seemed determined to make every second of work as hard as humanly possible for Kasie. She insisted on three coffee breaks before noon, and the pressing nature of the information coming in by fax kept Kasie working long after Pauline called it a day at three in the afternoon and went home. If Mrs. Charters hadn't helped out by letting Bess and Jenny make cookies, Kasie wouldn't have been able to do as much as she did.

She'd only just finished the new computer entries when Gil came in, dusty and sweaty and half out of humor. He didn't say a word. He went to the liquor cabinet and poured himself a scotch and water, and he drank half of it before he even looked at Kasie.

It took her a minute to realize that he was openly glaring at her.

"Is something wrong?" she asked uneasily.

"Pauline called me on the cell phone a few minutes ago. She said you're making it impossible for her to do her job," he replied finally.

Her heart skipped. So that was how the other woman was going to make points—telling lies.

"I've been showing her how to key in this data, and that's all I've done," Kasie told him quietly. "She hates the computer."

"Odd that she's done so well with it up until now," he said suspiciously.

"Debbie did well with it," Kasie replied bluntly, flushing a little at his angry tenseness. "She was apparently having to put her own work as well as Pauline's into the computer."

He took another sip of the drink. He didn't look convinced. "That isn't what Pauline says," he told her. "And I want to know why you suddenly want my girls in a boarding school, after you've spent weeks behind my back and against instructions winning them over, so they're attached to you." He added angrily, "I meant it when I said I have no plans to marry. So if that changes your mind about wanting to take care of them, say so and I'll give you a reference and two weeks severance pay!"

He really did look ferocious. Kasie's head was spinning from the accusations. "Excuse me?"

He finished the drink and put the glass down firmly on the counter below the liquor cabinet. His pale eyes were glittery. "John and I spent six of the worst years of our lives at boarding school," he added unexpectedly. "I'm not putting my babies in any boarding school."

Kasie felt as if she were being attacked by invisible hands. She stood up, her mind reeling from the charges. Pauline had been busy!

"I haven't said anything about boarding school," she defended herself. "Pauline said . . ."

He held up a hand. "I know Pauline," he told her. "I've known her most of my life. She doesn't tell lies."

Boy, was he in for a shock a little further on down the road, she thought, but she didn't say anything else. She was already in too much trouble, and none of it of her own making.

She didn't say a word. She just looked at him with big, gray, wounded eyes.

He moved closer, his mind reeling from Pauline's comments about Kasie. He didn't want to believe that

Kasie was so two-faced that she'd play up to the girls to get in Gil's good graces and then want to see them sent off to boarding school. But what did he really know about her, after all? She had no family except an aunt in Billings, or so she said, and except for the information on her application that mentioned secretarial school, nothing about her early education was apparent. She was mysterious. He didn't like mysteries.

He stopped just in front of her, his face hard and threatening as he glared down at her.

"Where were you born?" he asked abruptly.

The question surprised her. She became flustered. "I, well, I was born in . . . in Africa."

He hadn't expected that answer, and it showed. *"Africa?"*

"Yes. In Sierra Leone," she added.

He frowned. "What were your parents doing in Africa?"

"They worked there."

"I see." He didn't, but she looked as if she hated talking about it. The mystery only deepened.

"Maybe you're right," she said, unnerved by his unexpected anger and the attack by Pauline, which made her look like a gold digger. "Maybe I'm not the best person to look after the girls. If you like, I'll hand in my notice . . . !"

He had her by both shoulders with a firm grip and the expression on his face made her want to back away.

"And just for the record, ten years isn't a generation!" he said through his teeth as he glared down a her. His gaze dropped to her soft, generous mouth an it was like lightning striking. He couldn't help him self. The memory of her body in his arms on the porc swing took away the last wisp of his willpower. H bent quickly and took that beautiful softness under hi hard lips in a fever of hunger, probing insistently a her tight mouth with his tongue.

Kasie, who'd never been kissed in any intimate wa even by Gil, froze like ice at the skillful, invasive int macy of his mouth. She couldn't believe what wa happening. Her hands against his chest clenched an she closed her eyes tightly as she strained against hi hold.

Slowly it seemed to get through to him that she wa shocked at the insistence. He lifted his demandin mouth and looked at her. This was familiar territor for him. But, it wasn't for her, and it was apparen After the way she'd responded to him the nigh before, he was surprised that she balked at a dee kiss. But, then, he remembered her chaste gowns an her strange attitude about wearing her beautiful hai loose. She wasn't fighting him. She looked . . strange.

His lean hands loosened, became caressing on he upper arms under the short sleeve of her dress. "I'r sorry. It's all right," he breathed as he bent again. " won't be rough with you. It's all right, Kasie . . ."

His lips barely brushed hers, tender now instead c demanding. A few seconds of tenderness brought sigh from her lips. He smiled against her soft mout as he coaxed it to part. He nibbled the full upper lip, tasting its velvety underside with his tongue, enjoying her reactions to him. He felt her young body begin to relax into his. She worked for him. She was an employee. He'd just been giving her hell about trying to trap him into marriage. So why was he doing this . . . ? She made a soft sound under her breath and her hands tightened on the hard muscles of his upper arms. His brows began to knit as sensation pulsed through him at her shy response. What did it matter *why* he was doing it, he asked himself, and threw caution to the winds.

His arms went around her, gently smoothing her against the muscular length of him, while his mouth dragged a response under its tender pressure. He felt her gasp, felt her shiver, then felt her arms sliding around his waist as she gave in to the explosion of warm sensation that his hungry kiss provoked in her.

It was like flying, he thought dizzily. He lifted her against him, feeding on the softness of her mouth, the clinging wonder of her arms around him. It had been years since a kiss had been this sweet, this fulfilling. Not since Darlene had he been so hungry for a woman's mouth. Darlene. Darlene. Kasie was so much like her . . .

Only the need to breathe forced him to put her down and lift his head. His turbulent eyes met her dazed ones and he had to fight to catch his breath.

"Why did you do that?" she asked unsteadily.

He was scowling. He touched her mouth with a lean forefinger. "I don't know," he said honestly. "Do you want me to apologize?" he added quietly.

"Are you sorry?" she returned.

"I am not," he said, every word deliberate as he stared into her eyes.

That husky statement made her tingle all over with delicious sensations, but he still looked formidable. His lean fingers caught her shoulders and gently moved her away. She looked as devastated as he felt.

Her eyes searched his quietly. She was shaking inside from the delicious crush of his mouth, so unexpected. "What did you mean, about ten years not being a generation?" she asked suddenly.

"You harp on my age," he murmured coolly, but he was still looking at her soft, swollen mouth. "You shouldn't tell Pauline things you don't want me to hear. She can't keep a secret."

"I wouldn't tell her my middle name," she muttered. "She hates me, haven't you noticed?"

"No, I hadn't."

"It would never have been my idea to send the girls to boarding school," she insisted. "I love them."

His eyebrows lifted. Kasie didn't appear to be lying. But Pauline had been so convincing. And Kasie was mysterious. He wanted to know why she was so secretive about her past. He wanted to know everything about her. Her mouth was sweet and soft and innocent, and he had to fight not to bend and take it again. She was nervous with him now, as she hadn't been before. That meant that the attraction was mutual. It made him feel a foot taller.

"Pauline wants to go down to Nassau for a few days

with the girls. I want you to come with us," he said abruptly.

She gaped at him. "She won't want me along," she said with conviction.

"She will when she has to start looking out for Bess and Jenny. Her idea of watching them is to let them do what they please. That could be disastrous even around a swimming pool."

She grimaced. It would be a horrible trip. "We'd have to fly," she said, hating the very thought of getting on an airplane. She'd lost everyone she'd ever loved in the air, and he didn't know.

"The girls like you," he persisted gently.

"I'd really rather not," she said worriedly.

"Then I'll make it an order," he said shortly. "You're coming. Have you got a current passport?"

"Yes," she said without thinking.

He was surprised. "I was going to say that if you didn't have one, a birth certificate or even a voter's registration slip would be adequate." He was suspicious. "Why do you keep a passport?"

"In case I get kidnapped by terrorists," she said, tongue in cheek, trying to put aside the fear of the upcoming trip.

He rolled his eyes, let her go and walked to the door. "We'll go Friday," he said. "Don't take much with you," he added. "We'll fly commercial and I don't like baggage claim."

"Okay."

"And stop letting me kiss you," he added with faint arrogance. "I've already made it clear that there's no future in it. I won't marry again, not even to provid the girls with a grown-up playmate."

"I do know that," she said, wounded by the word "But I'm not the one doing the grabbing," she pointe out.

He gave her an odd look before he left.

She could have told him that she didn't have muc to take anywhere, and she almost blurted out why sh was afraid of airplanes. But he was already out th door. She touched her mouth. She tasted scotc whiskey on her lips and she was amazed that sh hadn't noticed while he was kissing her. Why had h kissed her again? she wondered dazedly. The othe question was why had she kissed him back? Her hea was reeling with the sudden shift in their relationshi since the night before. Kissing seemed to be addictiv Perhaps she should cut her losses and quit right awa But that thought was very unpleasant indeed. Sh decided that meeting trouble head-on was so muc better than running from it. She had to conquer h fear and try to put the past behind her once and for al Yes, she would go to Nassau with him and the girls– and Pauline. It might very well put things into pe spective if she saw Pauline and Gil as a family, whil there was still time to stop her rebellious heart fro falling in love.

Kasie's seat was separated from Gil's, Pauline and the girls' by ten rows. Gil didn't appear please and he tried to change seat assignments, but it wasn possible. Kasie was rather relieved. She was uncon fortable with Gil since he'd kissed her so passion-ately.

Pauline was furious that Kasie had been included in the trip. She was doing everything in her power to get Kasie out of Gil's life, but nothing was going the way she planned. She'd envisioned just the four of them in the exquisite islands, where she could convince Gil that they should get married. He agreed to her suggestion about the trip more easily than she'd hoped, and then he said Kasie would have to come along to take care of the girls. He didn't even mention boarding school, as if he didn't believe Kasie had suggested it. Pauline was losing ground with him by the day. She could cheerfully have pushed Kasie out of the terminal window. Well, she was going to get rid of Miss Prim over there, whatever it took. One way or another, she was going to get Kasie out of Gil's house!

They boarded the plane, and Kasie smiled with false bravado as she passed the girls with a wave and found her window seat. There was only one seat next to hers. She was watching the people file in while she fought her own fear. Seconds later, a tall blond man wearing khakis swung into the seat beside hers and gave her an appreciative smile.

"And I thought this was going to be a boring flight," he chuckled as he stuffed his one carry-on bag under the seat in front of him and fastened his seat belt. "I'm Zeke Mulligan," he introduced himself with a smile. "I write freelance travel articles for magazines."

"I'm Kasie Mayfield," she replied, offering her

small hand with a wan smile. "I'm a governess to two sweet little girls."

"Where are the sweet little girls?" he asked with a grin.

"Ten rows that way," she pointed. "With their dad and his venomous secretary."

"Ouch, the jealousy monster strikes, hmm?" he asked. "Does she see you as competition?"

"That would be one for the books," she chuckled. "She's blond and beautiful."

"What are you, chestnut-haired and repulsive?" he chided. "Looks aren't everything, fellow adventurer."

"Adventuress," she corrected. She glanced out the window and noticed the movement of the motorized carts away from the plane. It was going to take off soon. Sure enough, she heard the rev of the engines and saw the flight attendants take up their positions to demonstrate the life vests even as the plane started to taxi out of its concourse space. "Oh, gosh," she groaned, tightening her hands on the arms of her seat.

"Afraid of flying?" he asked gently.

"I lost my family in a plane crash," she said in a rough whisper. "This is the first time I've flown, since I lost them. I don't know if I can . . . !"

She'd started to pull at her seat belt. He caught her hand and stilled it. "Listen to me," he said gently, "air travel is the safest kind. I've been knocking around on airplanes for ten years, I've been around the world three times. It's all right," he stressed, his voice low and deep and comforting. His fingers contracted around hers. "You just hold on to me. I'll get you through takeoff and landing. Once you've conquered the fear, you'll be fine."

"Are you sure?" she asked on a choked laugh.

"I walked away from a crash once," he told her quietly. "A week later I had to get on a plane for Paris. Yes," he added. "I'm sure. If I could do it, I know you can."

Her lips parted as she let out the breath she'd been holding. He was nice. He was very nice. He made her feel utterly safe. She clung to his hand as the airplane taxied to the runway and the pilot announced that they were next in line to take off.

"Here we go," her seat companion said in her ear. "Think of *Star Trek* when the ship goes into light speed," he added on a chuckle. "Think of it as being flung up into the stars. It's exciting. It's great!"

She held on tighter as the plane taxied onto the runway, revved up its engines and began to pick up speed.

"We can even sing the Air Force song as we go," he said. "I spent four years in it, so I can coach you if you can't remember the words. Come on, Kasie. Sing!"

Kasie started to hum the words of the well-known song.

The passengers around them noticed Kasie's terror and her companion's protective attitude, and suddenly they all started singing the Air Force song. It diverted Kasie with uproarious laughter as the big airplane shot up into the blue sky, leaving her stomach and her fears far behind.

"I'm very grateful," she told him when they were

comfortably leveled off and the flight attendants were getting the refreshment cart ready to take down the aisle. "You can't imagine how terrified I was to get on this plane."

"Yes, I can. I'm glad I was here. Where are you staying in Nassau?" he added.

She laughed. "I'm sorry. I don't know! I didn't realize that until just now. My boss will have all the details in hand, and a driver to meet us when we land. I didn't ask."

"New Providence is a small island," he told her. "We'll see each other again. I'm at the Crystal Palace on Cable Beach. You can phone me if you get a few free minutes and we'll have lunch."

"Do you go overseas to do stories?" she asked.

He nodded. "All over the world. It's a great job, and I actually get paid to do it." He leaned close to her ear. "And once, I worked for the CIA."

"You didn't!" she exclaimed, impressed.

"Just for a year, while I was in South America," he assured her. "I might have kept it up, but I was married then and she didn't want me taking chances, especially while she was carrying our son."

"She doesn't travel with you?" she asked curiously.

"She died, of a particularly virulent tropical fever," he said with a sad smile. "My son is six, and I leave him with my parents when I have to go away during his school year. During the summer, he goes places with me. He loves it, too."

He pulled out his wallet and showed her several photographs of a child who was his mirror image.

"His name's Daniel, but I call him Dano."

"He really is cute."

"Thanks."

The flight attendant was two rows away, with snack meals and drinks. Kasie settled down to lunch with no more reservations. She'd landed on her feet. She wondered what Gil would think if he saw her with this nice young man. Nothing, probably, she thought bitterly, not when he was so wrapped up in Pauline. Well, she wasn't going to let that spoil her trip.

Nassau was unexpected. Kasie fell in love with it on first sight. She'd seen postcards of the Bahamas, and she'd always assumed that the vivid turquoise and sapphire color of the waters was exaggerated. But it wasn't. Those vivid, surreal colors were exactly what the water looked like, and the beaches were as white as sugar. She stared out the window of the hired car with her breath catching in her chest. She'd gone overseas with her parents as a child, but to distant and primitive places. She remembered the terror of those places far better than she remembered the scenery, even at so young an age. Even now, it was hard to think about how she'd lost the parents who'd loved her and Kantor so much. It was harder to think of Kantor . . .

"Do stop pressing your nose against the glass, Kasie. You look about Jenny's age!" Pauline chided from her seat beside Gil.

"That's funny," Bess said with a giggle, not understanding the words were meant to hurt.

"I've never seen anything so beautiful," Kasie murmured a little shyly. "It really does look like paradise."

Pauline yawned. Gil ignored her and watched Kasie a little irritably as she and the girls enthused over the beach.

"When can we go swimming in the ocean, Daddy?" Bess asked excitedly.

"We have to check into the hotel first, baby," Gil told her. "And even then, the beach is dangerous. Kasie doesn't swim."

"Oh, we can take them with us," Pauline said lazily. "I'll watch them."

It occurred to Gil that he never trusted Pauline with his children. She wasn't malicious, she just didn't pay attention to what they were doing. She'd be involved in putting on sunscreen and lying in the sun, not watching children who could become reckless. Bess was especially good at getting into trouble.

"That's Kasie's job," Gil said, and put a long arm around Pauline just to see the reaction it got from Kasie. It was a constant source of anger that he couldn't keep his hands off Kasie when he was within five feet of her, and he still didn't trust her.

Kasie averted her eyes. Odd, how much it hurt to see Pauline snuggle close to Gil as if she were part of him. Remembering the hungry, masterful way he'd kissed her in the study, Kasie flushed. She knew things about Gil Callister that she shouldn't know. He made her hungry. But he was showing her that he didn't feel the same way. It was painfully obvious what his relationship was with Pauline. Even though she'd guessed, it hurt to have it pointed out to her like this.

She knew then that she was going to have to resign her job when they got back to the States. If he married Pauline, there was no way she could live under the same roof with them.

Gil saw the reaction that Kasie was too young to hide, and it touched him. She felt something. She was jealous. He could have cheered out loud. It didn't occur to him then why he was so happy that Kasie was attracted to him.

"Who was the man you were talking to on the concourse, Kasie?" Gil asked unexpectedly.

"His name was Zeke," she replied with a smile. "He had the seat next to mine."

"I noticed him. He's good-looking," Pauline said. "What does he do?"

"He's a freelance writer for several travel magazines," Kasie told her. "He's down here doing a story on a new hotel complex."

Gil didn't look pleased. "Apparently you made friends quickly."

"Well, yes," she confessed. "I was a little nervous about flying. He talked to me while we got airborne." She grinned. "Didn't you hear us all singing the Air Force song?"

"So that's what it was," Pauline scoffed. "Good Lord, I thought the plane was full of drunks."

"Why were you afraid of flying?" Gil persisted.

Kasie averted her eyes to the girls. "My family die in an airplane crash," she said, without mentionin under what circumstances.

He shifted uncomfortably and looked at his daugh ters, who were watching for exciting little glimpses c people playing in the surf on the white beaches as the passed them.

"I'm all right now," she said. "The flight wasn't s bad."

"Not with a handsome man to hold your hand, Pauline teased deliberately.

"He *was* handsome," Kasie agreed, but withou enthusiasm, and without noticing that Gil's eyes wer beginning to glint with anger. He leaned back, glarin at Kasie.

She wondered what she'd done to provoke tha anger. It made her uneasy. Pauline obviously didn like it, either, and the woman was giving Kasie look that promised retribution in the near future. Kasi had a feeling that Miss Raines would make a ver bad enemy, and deep in her stomach, she felt ic cold.

Chapter 7

It took an hour to get checked into the luxury hotel. The girls played quietly in the marble-floored lobby with a puzzle book Kasie had brought along for them, while Pauline complained loudly and nonstop about the inconvenience of having to wait for a room to be made ready. By the time the clerk motioned them to the desk, Gil was completely out of humor. He hadn't smiled since they got off the plane, in fact. When they were given keys to a two-bedroom suite and a single adjoining room, Pauline's expression lightened.

"Oh, that's nice of you, darling, letting Miss Mayfield have a room of her own."

Gil gave her a look that combined exasperation with impatience. "The girls can't be alone at night in a strange hotel," he said curtly. "Kasie's staying in the room with them, and the other bedroom in the suite is mine. You get the single."

"Why can't I just share with you, darling?" Pauline purred, enjoying Kasie's sudden flush.

Gil looked furious. He glared down at her from his superior height. "Maybe you've forgotten that I don't move with the times," he said quietly.

Pauline laughed a little nervously. "You're kidding. What's so bad about two . . . friends sharing a room?"

"I'm not kidding," Gil said flatly. He handed Pauline her key and motioned for Kasie and the girls to follow him.

Pauline stomped into the elevator, fuming. She gave Kasie a ferocious glare before she folded her arms over her chest and leaned back against the wall. The bellboy signaled that he'd wait for the next elevator to bring their luggage up, because six other people had jumped into the elevator right behind Pauline.

Gil and Pauline led the way down the hall, with Kasie and the girls following suit.

"At least, you can take me out tonight," Pauline told Gil, "since Kasie's along to baby-sit. Come on, darling, please? They have the most beautiful casino over on Paradise Island, and floor shows, too."

"All right," he said. "Let me get the girls and Kasie settled first, and find out about room service. You will want to have supper up here, won't you?" he asked Kasie stiffly.

"Of course," she said, not wanting to make things worse than they were—if that was possible.

"Good. Kasie can take the girls out to the beach while I check with the concierge about reservations," he added, watching Pauline's face beam. "I'll pick you up at your room at five-thirty."

"But that only gives me an hour to dress," she moaned.

"You'd look beautiful in a pillowcase, and you know it," he chided. "Go on."

"Okay." Pauline walked off to her own room without a word to the girls or Kasie.

Gil opened the door, noting that the bellboy was coming down the hall toward them with the luggage on a rolling carrier. He motioned Kasie and the girls inside.

"The bedrooms both have two double beds," he told Kasie stiffly. "And there's a balcony off the sitting room, if you want to sit outside and watch the surf after the girls get to sleep," he added, indicating the French doors that led onto a small balcony with two padded chairs.

"We'll be fine," she told him.

"Don't let them stay up past eight, no matter what they say," he told her. "And don't you stay up too late, either."

"I won't."

He hesitated at the door to his own room and looked at Kasie for a long moment, until her heart began to race. "You didn't tell me that you lost your family in an air crash. Why?"

"The subject didn't come up," she said gruffly.

"If it had," he replied curtly, "you wouldn't have been sitting alone, despite Pauline's little machinations with the seat assignments."

She was taken aback by the anger in his tone. "Oh."

"You make me feel like a gold-plated heel from time to time, Kasie," he said irritably. "I don't like it."

"I was all right," she assured him nervously. "Zeke took care of me."

That set him off again. "You're getting paid to take care of my children, not to holiday with some refugee from a press room," he pointed out, his voice arctic.

She stiffened. "I hadn't forgotten that, *Mr.* Callister," she added deliberately, aware that the girls had stopped playing and were staring up at the adults with growing disquiet. She turned away. "Come on, babies," she said with a forced smile. "Let's go change into our bathing suits, then we can go play on the beach!"

"All of you stay out of the water," Gil said shortly. "And I want you back up here before I leave with Pauline."

"Yes, sir," Kasie said, just because she knew it made him angry.

He said something under his breath and slammed the door to his own room behind him. Kasie had a premonition that it wasn't going to be much of a holiday.

She and the girls played in the sand near the ocean. On the way outside, Kasie had bought them small plastic buckets and shovels from one of the stores in the arcade. They were happily dumping sand on each other while, around them, other sun-worshipers lay on towel-covered beach chaise lounges or splashed in the water. The hotel was near the harbor, as well, and they watched a huge white ocean liner dock. It was an exciting place to visit.

Kasie, who'd only ever seen the worst part of foreign countries, was like a child herself as she gazed with fascination at rows of other luxury hotels on the beach, as well as sailboats and cruise ships in port. Nassau was the brightest, most beautiful place she'd ever been. The sand was like sugar under her feet, although hot enough to scorch them, and the color of the water was almost too vivid to believe. Smiling, she drank in the warmth of the sun with her eyes closed.

But it was already time to go back up to the room. She hated telling the girls, who begged to stay on the beach.

"We can't, babies," she said gently. "Your dad said we have to be in the room when he leaves. There's a television," she added. "They might have cartoons."

They still looked disappointed. "You could read us stories," Bess said.

Kasie smiled and hugged her. "Yes, I could. And I will. Come on, now, clean out your pails and shovels, and let's go."

"Oh, all right, Kasie, but it's very sad we have to leave," Bess replied.

"Don't want to go." Jenny pouted.

Kasie picked her up and kissed her sandy cheek. "We'll come out early in the morning, and look for shells on the beach!"

Jenny's eyes lit up. She loved seashells. "Truly, Kasie?"

"Honest and truly."

"Whoopee!" Bess yelled. "I'll get Jenny's pail, too. Can we have fish for supper?"

"Anything you like," Kasie told her as she put Jenny down and refastened her swimsuit strap that had come loose.

Above them, at the window of his room, Gil watched the byplay, unseen. He sighed with irritation as he watched the girls respond so wholeheartedly to Kasie. They loved her. How were they going to react if she decided to quit? She was very young; too young to think of making a lifelong baby-sitter. Pauline said she'd been very adamant about sending the girls away to school, but that was hard to believe, watching her with them. She was tender with them, as Darlene had been.

He rammed his hands hard into the pockets of his dress slacks. It hurt remembering how happy the two of them had been, especially after the birth of their second little girl. In the Callister family, girls were special, because there hadn't been a girl in the lineage for over a hundred years. Gil loved having daughters. A son would have been nice, he supposed, but he wouldn't have traded either of his little jewels down there for anything else.

It wounded him to remember how cold he'd been to Kasie before and after the plane trip. He hadn't known about her family dying in a plane crash. He could only imagine how difficult it had been for her to get aboard with those memories. And he'd been sitting with Pauline, talking about Broadway shows. Pauline had said that Kasie wanted to sit by herself, so he hadn't protested.

Then, of course, there was this handsome stranger who'd comforted her on the flight to keep her from being afraid. He could have done that. He could have held her hand tight in his and kissed her eyes shut while he whispered to her . . .

He groaned out loud and turned away from the window. She was worming her way not only into his life and his girls' lives, but into his heart as well. He hadn't been able to even think about Pauline in any romantic way since Kasie had walked into his living room for the job interview. Up until then, he'd found the gorgeous blonde wonderful company. Now, she was almost an afterthought. He couldn't imagine why. Kasie wasn't really pretty. Although, she had a nice figure and a very kissable mouth and those exquisitely tender eyes . . .

He jerked up the phone and dialed Pauline's extension. "Are you ready to go?" he asked.

"Darling, I haven't finished my makeup. You did say five-thirty," she reminded him.

"It is five-thirty," he muttered.

"Give me ten more minutes," she said. "I'm going to make you notice me tonight, lover," she teased. "I'm wearing something very risqué!"

"Fine," he replied, unimpressed. "I'll see you in ten minutes."

He hung up on her faint gasp of irritation. He didn't care if she wore postage stamps, it wasn't going to cure him of the hunger for Kasie that was tormenting him.

He heard the suite door open and the sound of his children laughing. Strange how often they laughed these days, when they'd been so somber and quiet before. She brought out the best in people. Well, not in himself, he had to admit. She brought out the worst in him, God knew why.

He went out into the big sitting room, still brooding.

"Daddy, you look nice!" Bess said, running to him to be picked up and kissed heartily. "Doesn't he look nice, Kasie?" she asked.

"Yes," Kasie said, glancing at him. He was dishy in a tuxedo, she thought miserably, and Pauline probably looked like uptown New York City in whatever she was wearing. Pauline was like a French pastry, while Kasie was more like a stale doughnut. The thought amused her and she smiled.

"Bess, get the menu off the desk and take it in your room. You and Jenny decide what you want to eat," Gil told them.

"Yes, Daddy," Bess said at once, scooping up the menu and her sister's hand as they left the room.

"Don't let them fill up on sweets," he cautioned Kasie. His pale eyes narrowed on her body in the discreet, one-piece blue bathing suit she was wearing with sandals and a sheer cover-up in shades of blue. Her hair was down around her shoulders. She looked good enough to eat.

"I won't," she promised, moving awkwardly toward the bathroom with the towel she'd been sunbathing on.

"Next time, get a towel from the caretaker down on the beach," he said after she'd put the towel in the bathroom. "They keep them there for beach use."

She flushed. "Sorry. I didn't know."

He moved toward her. In flats, she was even shorter than usual. He looked down at her with narrow, stormy eyes. The curves of her pretty breasts were revealed in the suit and he thought for one insane instant of bending and putting his mouth right down on that soft pink skin.

"Mr. Callister," she began, the name almost choking

her as his nearness began to have the usual effect on her shaking knees.

His lean hand moved to her throat and touched it lightly, stroking down to her bare shoulder and then back to her collarbone. "You've got sand on your skin," he observed.

"We had a little trouble making a sand castle, so the girls covered me up instead," she said with an unsteady laugh.

His hand flattened on the warm flesh and he looked into her huge, soft eyes, waiting for a reaction. Her pulse became visible in her throat. His blood began to surge, hot and turbulent, in his veins. His fingers spread out deliberately, so that the touch became intimate.

She wasn't protesting. She hadn't moved an inch. She didn't even seem to be breathing as she looked up into his pale, glittery eyes and waited, spellbound, for whatever came next.

Without saying a word, his fingers slid under the strap that held up her bodice. They inched into the suit and traced exquisite patterns on the soft, bare flesh that had never been exposed to the sun, or to a man's eyes. He watched her lips part, her eyes dilate with fascination and curiosity.

His hand stilled as he realized what he was doing. The girls were right in the next room, for God's sake. Was he losing his mind?

He jerked his hand back as if he'd scalded it and his expression became icy. "You'd better change," he said through his teeth.

She didn't move. Her eyes were wide, curious, apprehensive. She didn't understand his actions or his obvious anger.

But he was suspicious of her. He didn't trust her, and he didn't like his unchecked response to her. She could be anybody, with any motive in mind. She dressed like a repressed woman, but she never resisted anything physical that he did to her. He began to wonder if she was playing up to him with marriage in mind—or at least some financially beneficial liaison. He knew that she wasn't wealthy. He was. It put him at a disadvantage when he tried to puzzle out her motives. He knew how treacherous some women could be, and he'd been fooled once in recent months by a woman out for what she could get from him. She'd been kind to the girls, too, and she'd played the innocent with Gil, leading him on until they ended up in her bedroom. Of course, she'd said then, they'd have to get married once they'd been intimate . . .

He'd left her before the relationship was consummated, and he hadn't called her again. Not that she'd given up easily. She'd stalked him until he produced an attorney and a warrant, at which point she'd given up the chase.

Now, he was remembering that bad experience and superimposing her image over Kasie's innocent-looking face. He knew nothing about her. He couldn't take the risk of believing what he thought he saw in her personality. She could be playing him for a sucker, very easily.

"You don't hold anything back, do you?" he asked

120

conversationally, and it didn't show that he'd been affected by her. "Are you like that all the way into the bedroom?" he added softly, so that the girls wouldn't hear.

Kasie drew in a long breath. "I wouldn't know," she said huskily, painfully aware that she'd just made an utter fool of herself. "I'll get dressed."

"You might as well, where I'm concerned," he said pleasantly. "You're easy on the eyes, Kasie, but in the dark, looks don't matter much."

She stared at him with confusion, as if she couldn't believe she was hearing such a blatant remark from him.

He slid his hands into his pockets and studied her arrogantly from head to toe. "You'd need to be prettier," he continued, "and with larger . . . assets," he said with a deliberate study of her pert breasts. "I'm particular about my lovers these days. It takes a special woman."

"Which, thank God, I'm not," she choked, flushing. "I don't sleep around."

"Of course not," he agreed.

She turned away from him with a sick feeling in her stomach. She'd loved his touch. It had been her first experience of passion, and it had been exquisite because it was Gil touching her. But he thought she was offering herself, and he didn't want her. She should be glad. She wasn't a loose woman. But it was a deliberate insult, and she wondered what she'd done to make him want to hurt her.

Her reaction made him even angrier, but he didn't

121

let it show. "Giving up so easily?" he taunted.

She kept her back to him so that he wouldn't see her face. "We've had this conversation once," she pointed out. "I know that you don't want to remarry, and I've told you that I don't sleep around. Okay?"

"If I catch you in bed with that hack writer, I'll fire you on the spot," he added, viciously.

She turned then and glared at him from wet eyes. "What's the matter with you?" she asked.

"A sudden awakening of reason," he said enigmatically. "You look after the girls. That's your job."

"I never thought it involved anything else," she said.

"And it doesn't," he agreed. "The fringe benefits don't include the boss."

"Some fringe benefit," she scoffed, regaining her composure. "A conceited, overbearing, arrogant rancher who thinks he's on every woman's Christmas list!"

He lifted an eyebrow over eyes with cynical sophistication gleaming in them. "Don't look for me under your Christmas tree," he chided.

"Don't worry, I won't." She turned and kept walking before he could say anything worse. Of all the conceited men on earth!

He watched her go with mixed emotions, the strongest of which was desire. She made him ache all over. He checked his watch. Pauline's ten minutes were up, and he wanted out of this apartment. He called a good-night to the girls and went out without another word to Kasie.

When he got back in, at two in the morning, he paused long enough to open Kasie's door and look in.

She was wearing another of those concealing cotton gowns, with the covers thrown off. Jenny was curled up against one shoulder and Bess was curled into the other. They were all three asleep.

Gil ground his teeth together just looking at the picture they made together. His girls and Kasie. They looked more like mother and daughters. The thought hurt him. He closed the door with a little jerk and went back into his own room. Despite Pauline's alluring gown and her spirited conversation, he had been morose all evening.

Pauline had noticed, and knew the reason. She was, she told herself, going to get rid of the competition. It only needed the right set of circumstances.

Fate provided them only two days later. Kasie and Gil were barely speaking now. She avoided him, and he did the same to her. If the girls noticed, they kept their thoughts to themselves. Impulsively Kasie phoned Zeke at his hotel and asked if he'd like to come over and have lunch with her at the hotel, since she couldn't leave the girls.

He agreed with flattering immediacy, and showed up just as Kasie was drying off the girls.

"Surely you aren't going to take them to lunch with you?" Pauline asked, laughing up at Zeke, who attracted her at once. "I'll watch them while you eat."

"Please can't we stay and play in the pool?" Bess asked Kasie. "Miss Raines will watch us, she said so."

123

"Please," Jenny added with a forlorn look.

"You'll be right inside, won't you?" Pauline asked cunningly. "Go ahead and enjoy your lunch. I'm not going anywhere."

For an instant, Kasie recalled that Gil didn't trust Pauline with the girls. But it was only for a few minutes and, as Pauline had said, they were going to be just inside the nearby restaurant that overlooked the pool.

"Well, all right then, if you really don't mind," she told Pauline. "Thank you."

"It's my pleasure. Have fun now," Pauline told her. "And don't worry. Gil's not going to be back for at least a half hour. He's at the bank."

Kasie brooded over it even while she and Zeke ate a delicious seafood salad. They were seated at a window overlooking the swimming pool, but a row of hedges and hibiscus obscured the view so that only the deep end of the pool could be seen from their table.

"Stop worrying," Zeke told her with a grin. "Honestly, you act as if they were your own kids. You're just the governess."

"They're my responsibility," she pointed out. "If anything happened to them . . ."

"Your friend is going to watch them. Now stop arguing and let me tell you about this new hotel and casino they're opening over on Paradise Island."

"Okay," she relented, smiling. "I'll stop brooding."

Outside by the pool, Pauline had noticed that Kasie and her companion couldn't see beyond the hedges.

She smiled coldly as she looked at the little girls. Jenny was sitting on the steps of the wading pool, playing with one of her dolls in the water.

Closer to Pauline, Bess was staring down at the swimming pool where the water was about six feet deep—far too deep for her to swim in.

"I wish I could dive," she told Pauline.

"But it's easy," Pauline told her, making instant plans. "Just put your arms out in front of you like this," she demonstrated, "and jump in. Really, it's simple."

"Are you sure?" Bess asked, thrilled that an adult might actually teach her how to dive!

"Of course! I'm right here. How dangerous can it be? Go ahead. You can do it."

Of course she could, Bess thought, laughing with delight. She put her arms in the position Pauline had demonstrated and shifted her position to dive in. There wasn't anybody else around the pool to notice if she did it wrong. She'd show her daddy when he came back. Wouldn't he be surprised?

She moved again, just as Pauline suddenly turned around. Her leg accidentally caught one of Bess's. Pauline fell and so did Bess, but Bess's head hit the pavement as she went down. The momentum kept her going, and she rolled into the pool, unconscious.

"Oh, damn!" Pauline groaned. She got to her feet and looked into the pool, aware that Jenny was screaming. "Do shut up!" she told the child. "I'll have to get someone . . ."

But even as she spoke, Gil came around the corner of the hotel, oblivious to what had just happened.

"Daddy!" Jenny screamed. "Bess falled in the swimmy pool!"

Gil didn't even break stride. He broke into a run and dived in the second he was close enough. He went to the bottom, scooped up his little girl and swam back up with all the speed he could muster. Out of breath, he coughed as he lifted Bess onto the tiles by the pool and climbed out himself. He turned the child over and rubbed her back, aware that she was still breathing by some miracle. She coughed and water began to dribble out of her mouth, and then to gush out of it as she regained consciousness.

"Call an ambulance," he shot at Pauline.

"Oh, dear, oh, dear," she murmured, biting her nails.

"Call a damned ambulance!" he raged.

One of the pool boys saw what was going on and told Gil he'd phone from inside the hotel.

"Where's Kasie?" Gil asked Pauline with hateful eyes as Jenny threw herself against him to be comforted. Bess was still coughing up water.

There it was. The opportunity. Pauline drew in a quick breath. "That man came by to take her to lunch. You know, the man she met on the plane. She begged me to watch the girls so they'd have time to talk."

Gil didn't say anything, but his eyes were very expressive. "Where is she?"

"I really don't know," Pauline lied, wide-eyed. "She didn't say where they were going. She was clinging to him like ivy and obviously very anxious to be alone with him," she added. "I can't say I blame her, he's very handsome."

126

"Bess could have died."

"But I was right here. I never left them," she assured him. "The girls mean everything to me. Here, let me have Jenny. I'll take care of her while you get Bess seen to."

"Want Kasie," Jenny whimpered.

"There, there, darling," Pauline said sweetly, kissing the plump little cheek. "Pauline's here."

"Damn Kasie!" Gil bit off, horrified at what might have happened. Kasie knew he didn't trust Pauline to watch the girls. Why had Kasie been so irresponsible? Was it to get back at him for what he'd said the night they arrived in Nassau?

When the ambulance arrived, Kasie and Zeke left their dessert half-eaten and rushed out the door. Zeke had to stop to pay the check, but Kasie, apprehensive and uneasy without knowing exactly why, rounded the corner of the building just in time to see little Bess being loaded onto the ambulance.

"Bess! What happened?!" Kasie asked, sobbing.

"She hit her head on the pool, apparently, and almost drowned, while you were away having a good time with your boyfriend," Gil said furiously. The expression on his face could have backed down a mob. "You've got a ticket home. Use it today. Go back to the ranch and start packing. I want you out of my house when I get back. I'll send your severance pay along, and you can thank your lucky stars that I'm not pressing charges!"

"But, but, Pauline was watching them—" Kasie began, horrified at Bess's white face and big, tragic

127

eyes staring at her from the ambulance.

"It was your job to watch them," Gil shot at her. "That's what you were paid to do. She could have died, damn you!"

Kasie went stark white. "I'm sorry," she choked, horrified.

"Too late," he returned, heading to the ambulance. "You heard me, Kasie," he added coldly. "Get out. Pauline, take care of Jenny until I get back."

"Of course, darling," she cooed.

"And get her away from the swimming pool!"

"I'll take her up to my room and read to her. I hope you'll be fine, Bess, darling," she added.

Kasie stood like a little statue, sick and alone and frightened as the ambulance closed up and rushed away, its lights flashing ominously.

Pauline turned and gave Kasie a superior appraisal. "It seems you're out of a job, Miss Mayfield."

Kasie was too sick at heart to react. She didn't have it in her for a fight. Seeing Bess lying there, so white and fragile was acutely painful. Even Jenny seemed not to like her anymore. She buried her face against Pauline and clung.

Pauline turned and carried the child back to her chaise lounge to get her room key. Not bad, she thought, for a morning's work. One serious rival accounted for and out of the way.

Zeke caught up with Kasie at the pool. "What happened?" he asked, brushing a stray tear from Kasie's cheek.

"Bess almost drowned," she said huskily. "Pauline

128

promised to watch her. How did she hit her head?"

"I wouldn't put much past that woman," he told Kasie somberly. "Some people won't tolerate rivals."

"I'm no rival," she replied. "I never was."

Having noted the expression on her boss's face at the airport when he'd said goodbye to Kasie, he could have disputed that. He knew jealousy when he saw it. The man had been looking at him as if he'd like to put a stake through his heart.

"He fired me," Kasie continued dazedly. "He fired me, without even letting me explain."

"Trust me, after whatever she told him, it wouldn't have done any good. Go home and let things cool down," he added. "Most men regain their reason when the initial upset passes."

"You know a lot about people," Kasie remarked as they started up to her room.

"I'm a reporter. It goes with the territory. I'll go with you to the airport and help you change the ticket," he added grimly. "Not that I want to. I was looking forward to getting to know you. Now we'll be ships that passed in the night."

"So we will. Do you believe in fate?" she asked numbly.

"I do. Most things happen for a reason. Just go with the flow." He grinned. "And don't forget to give me your home address! I won't be out of the country forever."

Chapter 8

It didn't take long for Kasie to pack. She wouldn't let herself think of what was ahead, because she'd cry, and she didn't have time for tears. She changed into a neat gray pantsuit to travel in, and picked up her suitcase and purse to put them by the door. But she stopped long enough to find the phone number of the hospital and check on Bess. The head nurse on the floor, once Kasie's relationship to the girls was made clear, told her that the child was sitting up in bed asking for ice cream. Kasie thanked her and hung up. She wondered if the news would have been quite as forthcoming if she'd mentioned that she'd just been fired.

She moved out into the sitting room with her heart like a heavy weight in her chest. She looked around to make sure she hadn't forgotten anything and went into the hall with her small piece of carry-on luggage on wheels and her pocketbook. It was the most painful moment of her recent life. She thought of never seeing the girls and Gil again, of having Gil hate her. Tears stung her eyes, and she dashed at them impatiently with a tissue.

As she passed Pauline's room, she hesitated. She wanted to say goodbye to little Jenny. But on second thought, she went ahead to the elevator, deciding that it would only make matters worse. Besides, Pauline was probably still at the hospital with Gil. She wished she knew what had really happened by the pool. She should never have left the girls with Pauline, despite the other woman's assurances that she'd look after them. Gil had said often enough that she was responsible for them, not Pauline. She should have listened.

Downstairs, Zeke was waiting for her. He put her small bag into the little car he'd rented at the airport and drove her to the airport to catch her flight.

At the hospital, Bess was demanding ice cream. Gil hugged her close, more frightened than he wanted to admit about how easily he could have lost her forever.

"I'm okay, Daddy," she assured him with a grin.

"Does your head hurt?" he asked, touching the bandage the doctor had placed over the cut, which had been stitched.

"Only a little. But ice cream would make it feel better," she added hopefully.

"I'll see what I can do," he promised with a strained smile.

The nurse came in, motioning Pauline and Jenny in behind her. "I thought it might help to let her sister see her," she told Gil confidentially.

"Hi, Bess," Jenny said, sidling up to the bed. "Are you okay?"

"I'm fine," Bess assured her. "But it was real scary." She glared at Pauline. "It was your fault. You tripped me."

"Bess!" Gil warned his daughter while wondering at

Pauline's odd expression.

"I did not trip you!" Pauline shot back.

"You did so," Bess argued. "I wouldn't dive in, and you tripped me so I'd fall in."

"She's obviously delirious," Pauline said tautly.

"You told Kasie you'd stay right with us," she continued angrily. "And she told us not to go swimming, but you showed me how to dive and you told me to dive into the pool. And when I didn't, you tripped me!"

Pauline was flushed. Gil was looking vaguely murderous. "She did hit her head, you know," she stammered. "I was telling her how to dive, I didn't tell her to actually do it!"

"You tripped me and I hurt myself!" Bess kept on.

Pauline backed away from Gil. "What do I know about kids?" she asked impatiently. "She said she wanted to learn how to swim. I showed her a diving position. Then I slipped on the wet tiles and fell against her. It was an accident. I never meant to hurt her. You must know that I wouldn't deliberately hurt a child!" she added fiercely.

He was still silent, as the fear for Bess began to fade and his reason came back to him.

Pauline grabbed up her purse. "I was just trying to do Kasie a favor," she muttered. "That reporter wanted to take her to lunch and I told her to go ahead, that I'd watch the kids. Besides, she was just in the restaurant next to the pool!"

Gil felt his stomach do a nosedive. So Kasie hadn't deserted the kids. Pauline had told her to go,

132

and she'd been right inside. He'd fired Kasie, thinking she was at fault!

"I imagine that reporter went home with her," Pauline continued deliberately. "They were all over each other when he came to pick her up. Besides, governesses are thick on the ground. It won't be hard to replace her."

"Or you," he said coldly.

She looked shocked. "You can't mean you're firing me?"

"I'm firing you, Pauline," he said, feeling like a prize idiot. Kasie was gone, and it was as much Pauline's fault as it was his own. He knew she didn't like Kasie. "I need a full-time secretary. We've discussed this before."

She started to argue, but it was obvious that there was no use in it. She might still be able to salvage something of their relationship, just the same, if she didn't make a scene. "All right," she said heavily. "But we might as well enjoy the vacation, since we're here."

His face became hard. He thought of Kasie going back to Montana, packing, leaving. For an instant he panicked, thinking that she might go so far away that he'd never find her.

Then he remembered her aunt in Billings. Surely she wouldn't be that hard to locate. He'd give it a few days, let Kasie get over the anger she must be feeling right now. Maybe she'd miss the girls and he could persuade her to come back. God knew, she wouldn't miss him, he thought bitterly. He'd probably done more damage than he could ever make up to her. But when they got back, he was going to try. Misjudging Kasie seemed to be his favorite hobby these days, he thought miserably.

"Yes," he told Pauline slowly. "I suppose we might as well stay."

Pauline had hardly dared hope for so much time with him. She was going to try, really try, to take care of the girls and make them like her.

"Bess, shall I go and ask if they have chocolate ice cream?" she asked, trying to make friends. "I'm really sorry about accidentally knocking you into the pool."

"I want Kasie," Bess muttered.

"Kasie's gone home," Gil said abruptly, not adding that he'd fired her.

"Gone home?" Bess's face crumpled. "But why?"

"Because I told her to," he said shortly. "And that's enough about Kasie. We're going to have a good time . . . Oh, for God's sake, don't start bawling!"

Now it wasn't just Bess crying, it was Jenny, too. Pauline sighed heavily. "Well, we're going to have a very good time, aren't we?" she said to nobody in particular.

Mama Luke never pried or asked awkward questions. She held Kasie while she cried, sent her to unpack and made hot chocolate and chicken soup. That had always been Kasie's favorite meal when she was upset.

Kasie sat down across from her at the small kitchen table that had a gaily patterned tablecloth decorated with pink roses and sipped her soup with a spoon.

"You don't have to say a word," Mama Luke told her gently, and smiled. She had eyes like her sister, Kasie's mother, dark brown and soft. She had dark hair, too, which she kept short. Her hands, around the mug, were thin and wrinkled now, and twisted with arthritis, but they were loving, helping hands. Kasie had always envied her aunt her ability to give love unconditionally.

"I've been a real idiot," Kasie remarked as she worked through her soup. "I should never have let Pauline look after the girls. She isn't really malicious, but she's hopelessly irresponsible."

"You haven't had a man friend in my recent memory," Mama Luke remarked. "I'm sure you were flattered to have a handsome young man want to take you out to lunch."

"I was. But that doesn't mean that I should have let Pauline talk me into leaving the girls with her. Bess could very easily have drowned, and it would have been my fault," she added miserably.

"Give it time," the older woman said gently. "First, let's get you settled in. Then you can help me with the garden," she added with a grin.

Despite her misery, Kasie laughed. "I see. You're happy to have me back because I'm free labor."

Mama Luke laughed, too. It was a standing joke, the way she press-ganged even casual visitors into taking a turn at weeding the garden. She prescribed it as the best cure for depression, misery and anxiety. She was right. It did a lot to restore a good mood.

135

In the days that followed, Kasie worked in the garden a lot. She thought about Gil, and the hungry way he'd kissed her. She thought about the girls and missed them terribly. She'd really expected Gil to phone her. He knew she had an aunt in Billings, and it wouldn't have taken much effort for him to track her down. In fact, she'd put Mama Luke's telephone number down on her job application in case of emergency.

The thought depressed her even more. He knew where she'd be, but apparently he was still angry at her. God knew what Pauline had said at the hospital about how the accident happened. She'd probably blamed the whole thing on Kasie. Maybe the girls blamed her, too, for leaving them with Pauline, whom they disliked. She'd never felt quite so alone. She thought of Kantor and grew even sadder.

Mama Luke came out into the garden and caught her brooding. "Stop that," she chided softly. "This is God's heart," she pointed out. "It's creation itself, planting seed and watching little things grow. It should cheer you up."

"I miss Bess and Jenny," she said quietly, leaning on her hoe. She was dirty from head to toe, having gotten down in the soil to pull out stubborn weeds. There was a streak of it across her chin, which Mama Luke wiped off with one of the tissues she always carried in her pocket.

"I'm sure they miss you, too," the older woman assured her. "Don't worry so. It will all come right. Sometimes we just have to think of ourselves as

136

leaves going down a river. It's easy to forget that God's driving."

"Maybe He doesn't mind back seat drivers," Kasie said with a grin.

Mama Luke chuckled. "You're incorrigible. Almost through? I made hot chocolate and chicken with rice soup."

"Comfort food." Kasie smiled.

"Absolutely. Stop and eat something."

Kasie looked at the weeding that still had to be done with a long sigh. "Oh, well, maybe the mailman has some frustrations to work off. He's bigger than I am. I'll bet he hoes well."

"I'll try to find out," she was assured. "Come on in and wash up."

It was good soup and Kasie had worked up an appetite. She felt better. But she still hated the way she'd left the Callister ranch. Probably everybody blamed her for Bess's accident. Especially the one person from whom she dreaded it. "I guess Gil hates me."

The pain in those words made Mama Luke reach out a gentle hand to cover her niece's on the table. "I'm sure he doesn't," she contradicted. "He was upset and frightened for Bess. We all say things we shouldn't when our emotions are out of control. He'll apologize. I imagine he'll offer you your job back as well."

Kasie shifted in the chair. "It's been a week," she said. "If he were going to hire me back, he'd have been in touch. I suppose he still believes Pauline and thinks he's done the best thing by firing me."

"Do you really?" Her aunt pursed her lips as her keen ears caught the sound of a car pulling up in the driveway. "Finish your hot cocoa, dear. I'll go and see who that is driving up out front."

For just a few seconds, Kasie hoped it would be Gil, come to give her back her job. But that would take a miracle. Her life had changed all over again. She was just going to have to accept it and get a new job. Something would turn up somewhere, surely.

She heard voices in the living room. One of them was deep and slow, and she shivered with emotion as she realized that she wasn't dreaming. She got up and went into the living room. And there he was.

Gil stopped talking midsentence and just looked at Kasie. She was wearing old jeans and a faded T-shirt, with her hair around her shoulders. He'd missed her more than he thought he could miss anyone. His heart filled with just the sight of her.

"I believe you, uh, know each other," Mama Luke said mischievously.

"Yes, we do," Kasie said. She recalled the fury in his pale eyes as he accused her of causing Bess's accident, the fury as he fired her. It was too painful to go through again, and he didn't look as if he'd come to make any apologies. She turned away miserably. "If you'll excuse me, I have to clean up," she called over her shoulder.

"Kasie . . . !" Gil called angrily.

She kept walking down the hall to her room, and she closed and locked the door. The pain was just too much. She couldn't bear the condemnation in his eyes.

Gil muttered under his breath. "Well, so much for wishful thinking," he said almost to himself.

"Come along and have some hot cocoa, Mr. Callister," Mama Luke said with a gentle smile. "I think you and I have a lot to talk about."

He followed her into the small, bright kitchen with its white and yellow accents. She motioned him into a chair at the table while she poured the still-hot cocoa into a mug and offered it to him.

"I'm Sister Luke," she introduced herself, noting his sudden start. "Yes, that's right, I'm a nun. My order doesn't wear the habit. I work with a health outreach program in this community."

He sipped cocoa, feeling as if more revelations were in store, and that he wasn't going to like them.

She sipped her own cocoa. He was obviously waiting for her to speak again. He studied her quietly, his blue eyes troubled and faintly disappointed at Kasie's reception.

"She's still grieving," she told Gil. "She didn't give it enough time before she started back to work. I tried to tell her, but young people are so determined these days."

He latched on to the word. "Grieving?"

"Yes." Her dark eyes were quiet and soft as they met his. "Her twin, Kantor, and his wife and little girl died three months ago."

His breath caught. "In an airplane crash," he said, recalling what Kasie had said.

"Airplane crash?" Her eyes widened. "Well, I suppose you could call it that, in a manner of speaking.

Their light aircraft was shot down——"

"What?" he exploded.

She frowned. "Don't you know anything about Kasie?"

"No. I don't. Not one thing!"

She let out a whistle. "I suppose that explains some of the problem. Perhaps if you knew about her background . . ." She leaned back in her chair. "Her parents were lay missionaries to Africa. While they were working there, a rebel uprising occurred and they were killed." She nodded at his look of horror. "I had already taken my vows by then, and I was the only family that Kasie and Kantor had left. I arranged to have them come to me, and I enrolled them in the school where I was teaching, and living, at the time. In Arizona," she added. "Kantor wanted nothing more than to fly airplanes. He studied flying while he was in school and later went into partnership with a friend from college. They started a small charter service. There was an opportunity in Africa for a courier service, so he decided to go there and set up a second headquarters for the company. While he was there, he married and had a little girl, Sandy. She and Lise, Kantor's wife, came and stayed with Kasie and me while Kasie was going through secretarial school. Kantor didn't want them with him just then, because there was some political trouble. It calmed down and he came and rejoined his family. He wanted to bring everyone home to Africa."

She grimaced. "Kasie didn't want him to go back. She said it was too risky, especially for Lise and

Sandy. She adored Sandy . . ." She hesitated, and took a steadying breath, because the memory was painful. "Kantor told her to mind her own business, and they all left. That same week, a band of guerrillas attacked the town where he had his business. He got Lise and Sandy in the plane and was flying them to a nearby town when someone fired a rocket at them. They all died instantly."

"My God," he said huskily.

"Kasie took it even harder because they'd argued. It took weeks for her to be able to discuss it without breaking down. She'd graduated from secretarial college and I insisted that she go to work, not because of money, but because it was killing her to sit and brood about Kantor."

He wrapped both hands around the cocoa mug and stared into the frothy liquid. "I knew there was something," he said quietly. "But she never talked about anything personal."

"She rarely does, except with me." She studied him. "She said that your wife died in a riding accident and that you have two beautiful little girls."

"They hate me," he said matter-of-factly. "I fired Kasie." He shrugged and smiled faintly. "John, my brother, isn't even speaking to me."

"They'll get over it."

"They may. I won't." He wouldn't meet her eyes. "I thought I might persuade her to come back. I suppose that's a hopeless cause?"

"She's hurt that you misjudged her," she explained. "Kasie loves children. It would never occur to her to

141

leave them in any danger."

"I know that. I knew it then, too, but I was out of my mind with fear. I suppose I lashed out. I don't know much about families," he added, feeling safe with this stranger. He looked up at her. "My brother and I were never part of one. Our parents had a governess for us until we were old enough to be sent off to school. I can remember months going by when we wouldn't see them or hear from them. Even now," he added stiffly, "they only contact us when they think of some new way we can help them make money."

She slid a wrinkled hand over his. "I'm sorry," she said gently. She removed her hand and pushed a plate of cookies toward him. "Comfort food," she said with a gleeful smile. "Indulge yourself."

"Thanks." He bit into a delicious lemon cookie.

"Kasie says you love your girls very much, and that you never leave them with people you don't trust. She's hating herself because she did leave them against her better judgment. She blames herself for the accident."

He sighed. "It wasn't her fault. Not really." His eyes glittered. "She wanted to have lunch with a man she met on the plane. A good-looking, young man," he added bitterly. "Pauline admitted causing the accident, but I was hot because Kasie was upset about flying and I didn't know it until it was too late. She was sitting all by herself." His face hardened. "If I'd known what you just told me, we'd have gone by boat. I'd never have subjected her to an airplane ride. But Kasie keeps secrets. She doesn't talk about herself."

"Neither do you, I think," she replied.

He shrugged and picked up another cookie. "She looks worn," he remarked.

"I've had her working in my garden," she explained. "It's good therapy."

He smiled. "I work cattle for therapy. My brother and I have a big ranch here in Montana. We wouldn't trade it for anything."

"I like animals." She sipped cocoa.

So did he. He looked at her over the mug.

"Kasie mentioned she was named for the mercenary K.C. Kantor." She raised an eyebrow amusedly. "That's right. I'm not sure how much she told you, but when Jackie, her mother, was carrying her, there was a guerrilla attack on the mission. Bob, my brother-in-law, was away with a band of workers building a barn for a neighboring family. They'd helped a wounded mercenary soldier hide from the same guerrillas, part of an insurgent group that wanted to overthrow the government. He was well enough to get around by then, and he got Jackie out of the mission and through the jungle to where Bob was. Kasie and Kantor were born only a day later. And that's why she was named for K.C. Kantor."

"They both were named for him," he realized. "Amazing. What I've heard about Kantor over the years doesn't include a generous spirit or unselfishness."

"That may be true. But he pays his debts. He'd still like to take care of Kasie," she added with a soft chuckle. "She won't let him. She's as independent as

143

my sister used to be."

It disturbed him somehow that Kasie was cherished by another man who could give her anything she wanted. "He must be a great deal older than she is," he murmured absently.

"He doesn't have those kind of feelings for her," she said quietly, and there was pain in her soft eyes. "He missed out on family life and children. I think he's sorry about that now. He tried to get her to come and stay with him in Mexico until she got over losing her twin, but she wouldn't go."

"One of her other character references was a Catholic priest."

She nodded. "Father Vincent, in Tucson, Arizona. He was the priest for our small parish." She sighed. "Kasie hasn't been to mass since her brother died. I've been so worried about her."

"She mentioned taking the girls with her to church," Gil said after a minute. "If I can get her to come back to work for me, it might be the catalyst to help her heal."

"It might at that," she agreed.

Gil took another cookie and nibbled it. "These are good."

"My one kitchen talent," she said. "I can make cookies. Otherwise, I live on TV dinners and the kindness of friends who can cook."

He sipped cocoa and thought. "How can I get her to go back with me?" he asked after a minute.

"Tell her the girls are crying themselves to sleep at night," she suggested gently. "She misses Sandy even more than her twin. She and the little girl were very close."

"She's close to my girls," he remarked with a reminiscent smile. "If there's a storm or they get frightened in the night, I can always find them curled up in Kasie's arms." His voice seemed to catch on the words. He averted his eyes toward the hallway. "The light went out of the house when she left it."

She wondered if he even realized what he was saying. Probably not. Men seemed to miss things that women noticed at once.

"I'll go and get her," she said, pushing back her chair. "You can sit by my fishpond and talk with the goldfish."

"My uncle used to have one," he recalled, standing. "I haven't had one built because of the girls. When they're older, I'd like to put in another one."

"I had to dig it myself, and I'm not the woman I used to be. It's only a little over a foot deep. One of my neighbors gave me his used pond heater when he bought a new one. It keeps my four goldfish alive all winter long." She moved to the door. "It's just outside the back door, near the birdbath. I'll send Kasie out to you."

He went out, his hands in his pockets, thinking how little he'd known about Kasie. It might be impossible for them to regain the ground they'd lost, but he wanted to try. His life was utterly empty without her in it.

Mama Luke knocked gently at Kasie's door and

145

waited until it opened. Kasie looked at her guiltily.

"I was rude. I'm sorry," she told the older woman.

"I didn't come to fuss," Mama Luke said. She touched Kasie's disheveled hair gently. "I want you to go out and talk to Mr. Callister. He feels bad about the things he said to you. He wants you to go back to work for him."

Kasie gave her aunt a belligerent look. "In his dreams," she muttered.

"The little girls miss you very much," she said.

Kasie grimaced. "I miss them, too."

"Go on out there and face your problem squarely," Mama Luke coaxed. "He's a reasonable man, and he's had a few shocks today. Give him a chance to make it up to you. He's nice," she added. "I like him."

"You like everybody, Mama Luke," Kasie said softly.

"He's out by the goldfish pond. And don't push him in," she added with a wicked little smile.

Kasie chuckled. "Okay."

She took a deep breath and went down the hall. But her hands trembled when she opened the back door and walked outside. She hadn't realized how much she was going to miss Gil Callister until she was out of his life. Now she had to decide whether or not to risk going back. It wasn't going to be an easy decision.

Chapter 9

Gil was sitting on the small wooden bench over-looking the rock-bordered oval fishpond, his elbows resting on his knees as he peered down thoughtfully into the clear water where water lilies bloomed in pink and yellow profusion. He looked tired, Kasie thought, watching him covertly. Maybe he'd been away on business and not on holiday with Pauline after all.

He looked up when he heard her footsteps. He got to his feet. He looked elegant even in that yellow polo shirt and beige slacks, she thought. He wasn't at all handsome, but his face was masculine and he had a mouth that she loved kissing. She averted her eyes until she was able to control the sudden impulse to run to him. Wouldn't that shock him, she thought sadly.

He looked wary, and he wasn't smiling. He studied her for a long time, as if he'd forgotten what she looked like and wanted to absorb every detail of her.

"How are the girls?" she asked quietly. "Is Bess going to be all right?"

"Bess is fine," he replied. "She told me every-thing." He grimaced. "Even Pauline admitted that she'd told you to go and have lunch with what's-his-name, and she'd watch the girls. She said she slipped and tripped Bess. I imagine it's the truth. She's never been much of a liar, regardless of her faults," he returned, his voice flat, without expression. "They told me you phoned the hospital to make sure Bess was all right."

"I was worried," she said, uneasy.

He toyed with the change in his pocket, making it jingle. "Bess wanted you, in the hospital. When I told her you'd gone home, she and Jenny both started crying." The memory tautened his face. "For what it's worth, I'm sorry that I blamed you."

She'd never wanted to believe anything as much as that apology. But it was still disturbing that he'd accused her without proof, that he'd assumed Bess's accident was her fault. She wanted to go back in the house. But that wouldn't solve the problem. She had to try and forget. He was here and he'd apologized. They had to go from there. "It's all right," she said after a minute, her eyes on the fish instead of him. "I understand. You can't help it that you don't like me."

"Don't . . . like you?" he asked. The statement surprised him.

She toyed with the hem of her shirt. "You never wanted to hire me in the first place, really," she continued. "You looked at me as if you hated me the minute you saw me."

His eyes were thoughtful. "Did I?" He didn't want to pursue that line of conversation. It was too new, too disturbing, after having realized how he felt about her. "Why do you call your aunt Mama Luke?" he asked to divert her.

"Because when I was five, I couldn't manage Sister Mary Luke Bernadette," she replied. "She was Mama Luke from then on."

He winced. "That's a young age to lose both parents."

"That's why I know how Bess and Jenny feel," she told him.

His expelled breath was audible. "I've made a hell of a mess of it, haven't I, Kasie?" he asked somberly. "I jumped to the worst sort of conclusions."

She moved awkwardly to the other side of the fishpond and wrapped her arms around her body. "I wasn't thinking straight. I knew you didn't trust Pauline to take care of the girls, but I let myself be talked into leaving them with her. You were right. Bess could have drowned and it would have been my fault."

"Stick the knife right in, don't be shy," he said through his teeth. His blue eyes glittered. "God knows, I deserve it."

Her eyes met his, wide with curiosity. "I don't understand."

She probably didn't. "Never mind." He stuck his hands into his pockets. "I fired Pauline."

"But . . . !"

"It wasn't completely because of what happened in Nassau. I need someone full-time," he interrupted. "She only wanted the job in the first place so that she could be near me."

The breeze blew her hair across her mouth. She pushed it back behind her ear. "That must have been flattering."

"It was, at first," he agreed, "I've known Pauline for a long time, and her attention was flattering. However, regardless of how Bess fell into the water, Pauline didn't make a move to rescue her. I can't get over that."

Kasie understood. She'd have been in the pool seconds after Bess fell in, despite the fact that she couldn't swim.

His piercing blue eyes caught hers. "Yes, I know. You'd have been right in after her," he said softly, as if he'd read the thought in her mind. "Even if you'd had to be rescued as well," he added gently.

"People react differently to desperate situations," she said.

"Indeed they do." His eyes narrowed. "I want you to come back. So do the girls. I'll do whatever it takes. An apology, a raise in salary, a paid vacation to Tahiti . . ."

She shrugged. "I wouldn't mind coming back," she said. "I do miss the girls, terribly. But . . ."

"But, what?"

She met his level gaze. "You don't trust me," she said simply, and her eyes were sad. "At first you thought I was trying to get to you through the girls, and then you thought I wanted them out of the way. In Nassau, you thought I left them alone for selfish reasons, so that I could go on a lunch date." She smiled sadly. "You have a bad opinion of me as a governess. What if I mess up again? Maybe it would be better if we just left things the way they are."

The remark went through him like hot lead. He hadn't trusted Kasie because she was so mysterious about her past. Now that he knew the truth about her, knew of the tragedies she'd suffered in her young life, lack of trust was no longer going to be a problem. But how did he tell her that? And, worse, how did he make up for the accusations he'd made? Perhaps he could tell her the truth.

"The girls' last governess was almost too good to be true," he began. "She charmed the girls, and me, until we'd have believed anything she told us. It was all an act. She had marriage in mind, and she actually threatened me with my own children. She said they were so attached to her that if I didn't marry her, she'd leave and they'd hate me."

She blinked. "That sounds as if she was a little unbalanced."

He nodded, his eyes cold with remembered bitterness. "Yes, she was. She left in the middle of the night, and the next morning the girls were delighted to find her gone."

He shook his head. "She was unstable, and I'd left the kids in her hands. It was such a blot on my judgment that I didn't trust it anymore. Especially when you came along, with your mysterious past and your secrets. I thought you were playing up to me because I was rich."

It hurt that he'd thought so little of her. "I see."

"Do you? I hope so," he replied heavily, and with a smile. "Because if I go back to Medicine Ridge without you, I wouldn't give two cents for my neck. John's furious with me. He's got company. Miss Parsons glares at me constantly. Mrs. Charters won't serve me anything that isn't burned. The girls are the

151

worst, though," he mused. "They ignore me completely. I feel like the ogre in that story you read them at bedtime."

"Poor ogre," she said quietly.

He began to smile. He loved the softness of her voice when she spoke. For the first time since his arrival, he was beginning to think he had a chance. "Feeling sorry for me?" he asked gently. "Good. If I wear on your conscience, maybe you'll feel sorry enough to come home with me."

She frowned. "What did Mama Luke tell you?" she asked suddenly.

"Things you should have told me," he replied, his tone faintly acidic. "She told me everything, in fact, except why you don't like the water."

She stared down into the fishpond, idly watching the small goldfish swim in and out of the vegetation. "When I was five, just before my parents were . . . killed," she said, sickened by the memory, "one of my friends at the mission in Africa got swept into the river. I saw her drown."

"You've had a lot of tragedy in your young life," he said softly. He moved a step closer to her, and another, stopping when he was close enough to lift a lean hand and smooth his fingers down her soft cheek. "I've had my own share of it. Suppose we forget the past few weeks, and start over. Can you?"

Her eyes were troubled. "I don't know if it's wise," she said after a minute. "Letting the girls get attached to me again, I mean."

His fingers traced her wide, soft mouth. "It's too late

152

to stop that from happening. They miss you terribly. So do I," he added surprisingly. He tilted her chin up and bent, brushing his lips tenderly over her mouth. His heavy eyebrows drew together at the delight that shafted through him from the contact. "When I think of you, I think of butterflies and rainbows," he whispered against her mouth. "I hated the world until you came to work for John. You brought the light in with you. You made me laugh. You made me believe in miracles. Don't leave me, Kasie."

He was saying something, more than words. She drew back and searched his narrow, glittery eyes. "Leave . . . you?" she questioned the wording.

"You don't have an ego at all, do you?" he asked somberly. "Is it inconceivable that I want you back as much as my girls do?"

Her heart jumped. She'd missed him beyond bearing. But if she went back, could she ever be just an employee again? She remembered the hard warmth of his mouth in passion, the feel of his arms holding her like a warm treasure. She hesitated.

"I don't seduce virgins," he whispered wickedly. "If that wins me points."

She flushed. "I wasn't thinking about that!"

He smiled. "Yes, you were and that's the main reason I won't seduce you."

"Thanks a lot."

He cocked an eyebrow. "You might sound a little more grateful," he told her. "Keeping my hands off you lately has been a world-class study in restraint."

Her eyes widened. "Really?"

She was unworldly. He loved that about her. He loved the way she blushed when he teased her, the way she made his heart swell when she smiled. He'd been lonely without her.

"But I'll promise to keep my distance," he added gently. "If you'll just come back."

She bit her lower lip worriedly. She did need the job. She loved the girls. She was crazy about Gil. But there were so many complications . . .

"Stop weighing the risks," he murmured. "Say yes."

"I still think . . ."

"Don't think," he whispered, placing a long forefinger over her lips. "Don't argue. Don't look ahead. We're going to go home and you're going to read the girls to sleep every night. They miss their stories."

"Don't you read to them?" she asked, made curious by a certain note in his voice.

"Sure, but they're getting tired of *Green Eggs and Ham*."

"They have loads of other books besides Dr. Seuss," she began.

He glowered at her. "They hid all the other books, including *Green Eggs and Ham*, but at least I remember most of that story. So they get told it every night. Two weeks of that and I can't even look at ham in the grocery story anymore without gagging . . ."

She was laughing uproariously.

"This is not funny," he pointed out.

"Oh, yes, it is," she said, and laughed some more.

He loved the sound. It reminded him of wind chimes. His heart ached for her. "Come home before

154

I get sick of eggs, too."

"All right," she said. "I guess I might as well. I can't live here with Mama Luke forever."

"She's a character," he remarked with a smile. "A blunt and honest lady with a big heart. I like her."

"She must like you, too, or she wouldn't have threatened to have you break down my bedroom door."

He pursed his lips. "Nice to have an ally with divine connections."

"She does, never doubt it," she told him, laughing. "I'll just go throw a few things into my suitcase."

He watched her go with joy shooting through his veins like fireworks. She was coming back. He'd convinced her.

Now all he had to do was make her see him as something more than an intolerant, judgmental boss. That was not going to be the easiest job he'd ever tackled.

Kasie kissed Mama Luke goodbye and waited while she hugged Gil impulsively.

"Take care of Kasie," her aunt told him.

He nodded slowly. "This time, I'll do better at that."

Mama Luke smiled.

They got into his black Jaguar and drove away, with Kasie leaning out the window and waving until her aunt was out of sight.

Gil watched her eyes close as she leaned back against the leather headrest. "Sleepy?"

"Yes," she murmured. "I haven't slept well since I

came back from Nassau."

"Neither have I, Kasie," he said.

Her head turned and she looked at him quietly. It made her tingle all over. He was really a striking man, all lean strength and authority. She'd never felt as safe with anyone as she did with him.

He felt her eyes on him; warm, soft gray eyes that gave him pleasure when he met them. Kasie was unlike anyone he'd every known.

"Did Pauline finish keying in the herd records to the computer before she left?" she asked, suddenly remembering the chore that had been left when they went to Nassau.

"She hasn't been around since we came home," he said evasively. "I think she's visiting an aunt in Vermont."

She traced a line down the seat belt that stretched across her torso. "I thought you were going to marry her."

He had a good idea where she'd heard that unfounded lie. "Never in this lifetime," he murmured. "Pauline isn't domestic."

"She's crazy about you."

"The girls don't like her."

She pursed her lips. "I see."

He chuckled, glancing at her while they stopped for a red light. "Besides, after they found out that I'd fired you, they made Pauline's life hell. Their latest escapade was to leave her a nice present in her pocketbook."

"Oh, dear."

"It was a nonpoisonous snake," he said reassuringly. "But she decided that she'd be better off not visiting when the girls were around. And since they were always around . . ."

She shook her head. "Little terrors," she said, but in a tone soft with affection.

"Look who's talking," he said with a pointed glare.

"I've never put snakes in anybody's purse," she pointed out. "Well, not yet, anyway."

He gave her an amused glance. "Don't let the girls corrupt you."

She smiled, remembering how much fun she'd had with the little girls. It made her happy that they wanted her back. Except for her aunt, she was alone in the world. She missed being part of a whole family, especially on holidays like Christmas.

The light changed and he pulled back out into traffic. Conversation was scanty the rest of the way home, because Kasie fell asleep. The lack of rest had finally caught up with her.

She was jolted awake by a firm hand on her shoulder.

"Wake up. We're home," Gil said with a smile.

She searched his blue eyes absently for a moment before the words registered. "Oh." She unfastened her seat belt and got out as he did.

The girls were sitting on the bottom step of the staircase when the door opened and Kasie walked in with Gil.

"Kasie!" Bess cried, and got up to run and throw herself into Kasie's outstretched arms.

"Bess!" Kasie hugged her close, feeling tears sting her eyes. She was so much like Sandy.

Jenny followed suit, and Kasie ended up with two arms full of crying little girls. She carried them to the staircase and sat down, cuddling them both close. Her face was wet, but she didn't care. She loved these babies, far more than she'd realized. She held them and rocked them and kissed wet little cheeks until the sobs eased.

"You mustn't *ever* leave us again, Kasie," Bess hiccuped. "Me and Jenny was ever so sad."

"Yes, we was," Jenny murmured.

"Oh, I missed you!" Kasie said fervently as she dug into her pocket for a tissue and wiped wet eyes all around.

"We missed you, too," Bess said, burying her face in Kasie's shoulder while Jenny clung to her neck.

Gil watched them with his heart in his throat. They looked as if they belonged together. They looked like a family. He wanted to scoop all three of them up in his arms and hold them so tight they'd never get away.

While he was debating that, John came down the hall and spotted Kasie. He grinned from ear to ear. "You're back! Great! Now maybe Mrs. Charters will cook something we can eat again!"

"That's not a nice way to say hello," Kasie chided with a smile.

"Sure it is! What good is a man without his stomach?" John asked. He moved closer to Kasie and the girls and bent to kiss Kasie's wet cheek. "Welcome back! It's been like a ballpark in January. Nobody smiled."

"I'm happy to be back," Kasie said. "But what about all those herd records that need putting into the computer?" she asked, realizing that Gil never had answered her when she'd questioned him about them.

"Oh, those. It turns out that Miss Parsons is a computer whiz herself," he said to Kasie's amusement. "She's got everything listed, including the foundation bloodlines. And remember that Internet site you suggested? It's up and running. We're already getting three hundred hits a day, along with plenty of queries from cattlemen around the country!"

"I'm so glad," Kasie said sincerely.

"So are we. Business is booming. But the babies have been sad." He glanced at his older brother meaningfully. "We missed you."

"It's nice to be back," Kasie said.

"Are we ever going to have lunch?" John asked then. "I'm fairly starved. Burned eggs and bacon this morning didn't do a lot for my taste buds."

"Mine, either," Gil agreed. "Go tell Mrs. Charters Kasie's back and is having lunch with us," he suggested. "That might get us something edible, even if it's only cold cuts."

"Good thinking," John said, smiling as he went out to the kitchen.

"Our eggs wasn't burned," Bess pointed out.

"Mrs. Charters wasn't mad at you, sweetheart," Gil told her. "You two need to run upstairs and wash your hands and faces before we eat."

"Okay, if Kasie comes, too," Bess agreed.

Kasie chuckled as both girls grabbed a hand and coaxed her to her feet. "I gather that I'm to be carefully observed from now on, so I don't make a run for the border," she murmured to Gil.

"That's right. Good girls," Gil said, grinning. "Keep her with you so she doesn't have a chance to escape."

"We won't let her go, Daddy," Bess promised.

They tugged her up the staircase, and she went without an argument, waiting in their rooms while they washed their hands and faces.

"Daddy was real mad when we came home," Bess told Kasie. "So was Uncle Johnny. He said Daddy should go and get you and bring you home, but Daddy said you might not want to, because he'd been bad to you. Did he take away your toys, Kasie and put you into time-out?"

"Heavens, no," she said at once.

"Then why did you go away?" the child insisted. "Was it on account of Pauline said you left us alone? We told Daddy the truth, and Pauline went away. We don't like her. She's bad to us when Daddy isn't looking. He won't marry Pauline, will he, Kasie?"

"I don't think so," she said carefully.

"Me and Jenny wish he'd marry you," Bess said wistfully. "You're so much fun to play with, Kasie."

Kasie didn't dare say anything about marriage. "You can't decide things like that, sweetheart," she told Bess. "People don't usually marry unless they fall in love."

"Oh."

The child looked heartbroken. Kasie went down on her knees and caught Bess gently by the waist. "What do you want to do after we have lunch?" she asked, changing the subject.

"Could we swim in the pool?"

She'd forgotten that the family had a swimming pool. "I suppose so," she said, frowning. "But it's pretty soon after your accident, Bess. Are you sure you want to?"

"Daddy and me went swimming the day after we came home," Bess said matter-of-factly. "Daddy said I mustn't be afraid of the water, after I fell in, so he's giving me swimming lessons. I love to swim, now!"

So some good had come out of the accident. That was reassuring. "Let's go down and eat something. Then we have to wait a little while."

"I know. We can pick flowers while we wait, can't we? There's some pretty yellow roses in a hedge behind the swimming pool," Bess told her.

"I love roses," Kasie said, smiling. "But perhaps we'd better not pick any until someone tells us it's all right."

"Okay, Kasie."

They went downstairs and Kasie helped Mrs. Charters set the table. She was welcoming and cheerful about having Kasie back again. John talked easily to Kasie and the children. Gil didn't. He picked at his food and brooded. He watched Kasie, but covertly. She wondered what was going on in his mind to make him so unhappy.

He looked up and met Kasie's searching eyes, and

161

she felt her stomach fall as if she was on a roller coaster. Her hands trembled. She put them in her lap to hide them, but her heartbeat pounded wildly and her nervousness was noticeable. Especially to the man with the arrogant smile, who suddenly seemed to develop an appetite.

Chapter 10

For the next few days, Gil seemed to watch every move Kasie made. He was cordial with her, but there was a noticeable difference in the way he treated her since her return. He was remote and quiet, even when the family came together at mealtimes, and he seemed uncomfortable around Kasie. She noticed his reticence and understood it to mean that he was sorry for the way he'd treated her before. He didn't touch her at all these days, nor did he seem inclined to include her when he took the girls to movies and the playground, even though he asked her along. But she always refused, to the dismay of the children. She excused it as giving them some time alone with their father. Gil knew that wasn't the truth. It made matters worse.

John left Thursday for a conference that Gil had been slated to attend, and Gil stayed home. Kasie noticed that he seemed unusually watchful and he was always around the ranch even when he wasn't around the house. He didn't explain why. Kasie would have loved thinking that it was because he was interested in her, but she knew that wasn't the reason. There was more distance between them now than there had ever been before.

Mrs. Charters mentioned that there was some uneasiness among the cowboys because of a threat that had been made. Kasie tried to ask Gil about it. He simply ignored the question and walked away.

He was missing at breakfast early one Monday morning. The girls were sleeping late, so Kasie walked into the dining room and found only John at the table.

"Pull up a chair and have breakfast," he invited with a grin. "I have to move bulls today, so I'm having seconds and thirds. I have to keep up my strength."

"If you keep eating like that, you could carry the bulls and save gas," she said wickedly. "I thought you had to go to Phoenix to show a bull this week?"

He averted his eyes. "I thought I'd put it off for another couple of weeks." He sipped coffee and studied Kasie quietly. "There's a new Western showing at the theater downtown. How would you like to pack up the girls and go with me to see it?"

Her eyes lit up. "I'd love to," she said at once.

He grinned. "Okay. We'll go tomorrow night. I, uh, noticed that you don't like going to movies with my brother, even if the girls go along."

"I just thought he'd like some time alone with them," she hedged. "After all, I'm just the governess."

He poured himself more coffee before he replied. "That's a bunch of hogwash, Kasie."

She drew in a long breath. "He makes me uncomfortable," she said. "I always feel like he's biding his time, waiting for me to make another mistake or do something stupid."

He chuckled. "He doesn't lie in wait to ambush you," he said softly. "He meant it when he apologized, you know. He was sorry he misjudged you. Believe me, it's a rare thing for him to make a mistake like that. But he's had some hard blows from women in recent years."

"I felt really bad about what happened," she said with a wistful sadness in her eyes. "I should have remembered that he never trusted Pauline to look after the girls. I'd met this man on the plane, and he invited me to lunch. I liked him. He kept me from being afraid on the way to Nassau."

John's face sobered, and she realized that Gil must have told him about her past. "I'm sorry about your brother and his family," he said, confirming her suspicions. "Gil and I haven't really been part of a family since our uncle died."

"Don't you ever go to see your parents?" she asked curiously.

"There was a time when they offered an olive branch, but you know Gil," he said soberly. "He's slow to get over things, and he refused to talk to them. Maybe they did neglect us, but I never thought it was malicious. They had kids before they were ready to have them. Lots of people are irresponsible parents. But you can't hold grudges forever." He frowned. "On second thought, maybe Gil can."

She smiled and reached across the table to lay her

hand over his. "Maybe one day you can try again. It would be nice for the girls to have grandparents."

"The only ones they have left are our parents. Darlene's died years ago." He caught her hand in his and held it tight. "You make the hardest things sound simple. I like myself when you're around, Kasie."

She laughed gently. "I like you, too," she said.

"I never believed you had anything to do with Bess getting hurt," he said somberly. "Anyone could see how much you care about the girls."

"Thanks. It's nice to know that at least one grown-up person in your family believed I was innocent," she said, oblivious to the white-faced, angry man standing in the hall with an armload of pale pink roses. "It hurt terribly that Gil thought I'd ever put the girls at risk in any way, least of all by neglecting them. But it wasn't the first time he's accused me of ulterior motives. I should be used to it by now. I think he's sorry he rehired me, you know," she added sadly, clinging to his hand. "He looks through me when he isn't glaring at me."

"Gil's had some hard knocks with women," John repeated, letting go of her hand. "Just give him time to adjust to being wrong. He rarely is." He picked up a forkful of eggs. "If it's any consolation, he roared around here for two weeks like every man's nightmare before he went after you. He wanted you to have enough time to get over the anger and let him explain his behavior. He would have gone sooner, he said, but he wasn't sure he could get in the front door."

She remembered her lacerated feelings when she'd arrived at her aunt's house. "It would have been tricky, at that," she agreed. "He was the last person on earth I wanted to see when I first came back from Nassau."

Footsteps echoed out in the hall and a door slammed. Kasie frowned.

"Sounds like Gil's going to bypass breakfast again this morning," John remarked as he finished his eggs. "He doesn't have much of an appetite these days."

"I'll just check and make sure it isn't the girls," Kasie said.

"Suit yourself, but I know those footsteps. He only walks that way when he's upset. God help whatever cowboy he runs into on his way."

Kasie didn't reply. She walked into the hall and there, on the hall table, was an armload of pink roses with the dew still clinging to the silky, fragrant petals. It took a few seconds for her to realize that Gil must have heard every word she'd said. She groaned inwardly as she gathered up the roses. Well, that was probably the end of any truce, she thought. He'd think she couldn't forgive him, and that would make him even angrier. Unless she missed her guess, he was going to be hell to live with from now on.

She took the roses to the kitchen and found a vase for them, which she filled with water before she arranged the flowers in it. With a sigh, she took them upstairs to her room and placed them on the dresser. They were beautiful. She couldn't imagine what had possessed Gil Callister to go out and cut her a bouquet. But the gesture touched her poignantly.

Sure enough, when Gil came in early for supper, he was dusty and out of humor. He needed a shave. He glared at everybody, especially Kasie.

"Aren't you going to clean up first?" John asked, aghast, when he sat down to the table in his chaps.

"What for?" he muttered. "I've got to go right back out again." He reached for his coffee cup, which Mrs. Charters had just filled, and put cream in it.

"Is something wrong?" John asked then, concerned.

"We've got a fence down." His eyes met his brother's. "It wasn't broken through. It was cut."

John stared at the older man. "Another one? That makes two in less than ten days."

"I know. I can't prove it, but I know it was Fred Sims."

John nodded slowly. "That makes sense. One of the cowboys who was friendly with him said Sims hasn't been able to find another job since we fired him."

Gil's pale blue eyes glittered. "That damned dog could have bitten my babies," he said. "No way was he going to keep it here after it chased them onto the porch."

"Bad doggie," Jenny agreed.

Bess nodded. "We was scared, Daddy."

"Sims is going to be scared, if I catch him within a mile of my property," Gil added.

"Don't become a vigilante," John cautioned his older brother. "Call the sheriff. Let him handle it. That's what he gets paid to do."

"He can't be everywhere," Gil replied, eyes narrowed. "I want all the cowboys armed, at least with rifles. I'm not taking any chances. If he's brazen enough to cut fences and shoot livestock, he's capable of worse."

Kasie felt her heart stop. So that was why he'd been around the ranch so much lately. The man, Sims, had threatened vengeance. Apparently he was killing cattle as well as cutting fences to let them escape. She pictured Gil at the end of a gun and she felt sick all over.

"I'll make sure everyone's been alerted and prepared for danger," John agreed. "But you stay out of it. You're the one person around here that Sims would enjoy shooting."

"He'd be lucky to get off a shot," Gil replied imperturbably. He finished his meal and wiped his mouth. "I've got to get back out there. We haven't finished stringing wire, and it's not long until dark."

"Okay. I'll phone the vet about those carcasses we found. I want him to look for bullet wounds."

"Good idea."

Gil finished the last sip of his coffee in a grim silence that seemed to spread to the rest of the family. The girls, sensing hidden anger in the adults around them, excused themselves and went upstairs to play in their room while Mrs. Charters cleaned away the dishes. John went to make a phone call.

Gil got to his feet without looking at Kasie and started toward the front door. Kasie caught up with him on the porch. It was almost dark. The sky was fiery red and pink and yellow where the sun was setting.

"Thank you," she blurted out.

He stopped and turned. "For what?"

His hat was pulled low over his eyes, and she couldn't see the expression in them, but she was pretty sure that he was scowling.

She went closer to him, stopping half an arm's length away. "For the roses," she said hesitantly. "They're beautiful."

He didn't move. He just stood there, somber, quiet. "How do you know they were meant for you?" he drawled. "And how do you know I brought them?"

She flushed scarlet. She didn't know for sure, but she'd assumed.

He averted his eyes, muttering under his breath. "You're welcome," he said tersely.

"That man, Sims," she continued, worried. "The day you fired him, John said that he had a mean temper and that he carried a loaded rifle everywhere with him. You . . . you be careful, okay?"

She heard the soft expulsion of breath. He moved a step closer, his lean hands lifting her oval face to his. She could see the soft glitter of his blue eyes in the faint light from the windows.

"What do you care if I get myself shot?" he asked huskily. "I'm the one who sent you packing without even giving you the chance to explain what happened in Nassau."

"Pauline didn't like me," she said. "And you trusted her. I was just a stranger."

"Not anymore, Kasie," he said gruffly.

"I mean, you didn't know anything about me," she

169

persisted. She searched his eyes, feeling jolts of electricity flow into her at the exquisite contact. "I was upset and I behaved badly when you came to Mama Luke's. But deep inside, I didn't blame you for not trusting me."

His lean hands tightened on her face. "I've done nothing but torment you since the first day you came here," he bit off. "I didn't want you in my life, Kasie," he whispered as he bent toward her. "I still don't. But a man can only stand so much . . . !"

His mouth caught hers hungrily. His arms swallowed her up against him, so that not an inch of space separated them. For long, achingly sweet seconds, they clung to each other in the soft darkness.

He drew away from her finally and stood just looking at her in a tense, hot silence. His hands were firm around her arms, and she swayed toward him helplessly.

She felt her knees go shaky, as if they had jelly in them instead of bone and cartilage. "Look, I'm very old-fashioned," she began in a choked tone.

"I almost never make love to women on the floor of the front porch."

She stared at him dimly, only slowly becoming aware that he was smiling and the words were both affectionate and teasing.

A tiny laugh burst from her swollen lips, although the kiss had rattled her.

"That's better," he said. His eyes narrowed. "How do you feel about my brother?"

Her mind refused to function. "How do I what?"

"Feel about John," he persisted coolly. "When I asked you why you wanted this job, you said it was because John was a dish. I know you had a crush on him. How do you feel now?"

She was at a loss to know what to say. "I like . . . him," she blurted out. "He's been kind to me."

"Kinder than I have, for damned sure," he agreed at once. "And he believed you were innocent when I didn't."

She frowned. "You explained why."

His hands tightened on her arms and his lips flattened. "He's younger than I am, single and rich and easygoing," he said harshly. "Maybe he'd be the best thing that ever happened to you."

Her eyes widened. "Thank you. I've always wanted a big, strong man to plan my future for me."

He let her go abruptly, angry. "You said it yourself. I'm a generation older than you with a ready-made family."

She couldn't make heads or tails of what he was saying. Her mind was spinning as she looked up at him.

"Maybe you're what he needs, too," he added coldly. "Someone young and optimistic and intelligent."

"Are you going to buy the ring, too?"

He turned away. "That wasn't funny."

"I don't want to marry your brother. Thanks, anyway."

He kept walking.

She ran after him. "That man Sims has got a gun,"

she called. "Don't you dare go out there and get shot!"

He paused on the top step and looked back at her as if he had doubts about her sanity. "John's going out with me as soon as he finishes his phone calls."

"Great!" she exclaimed angrily. "I can worry about both of you all night!"

"Worry about my daughters," he told her bluntly. "That's your only responsibility here. You work for me, remember?"

"I remember," she replied irritably. "Do you?"

"Stay in the house with the girls until I tell you otherwise. I don't want any of you on the porch or in the yard until we settle this, one way or another."

He did think there was danger. She heard it in every word. "I won't let anything happen to Bess and Jenny. I promise."

He glared at her. "Can you shoot?"

She shook her head. "But I know how to dial 911."

"Okay. Keep one of the wireless phones handy, just in case."

She moved toward him another step, wrapping her arms tight around her body. "Have you got a cell phone?"

He indicated the case on his belt. That was when she noticed an old Colt .45 strapped to his other hip, under the denim shirt he was wearing open over his black T-shirt.

Her breath caught. Until that minute, when she saw the gun, it was a possibility. But guns were violent, chaotic, frightening. She bit her lower lip worriedly.

"I'll be late. Make sure you lock the doors before

you go upstairs. John and I have keys."

"I will," she promised. "You be careful."

He ignored the quiet command. He took one long, last look at her and went on down the steps to his pickup truck, which was parked nearby.

She stood at the top of the steps until he drove away, staring after him worriedly. She wanted to call him back, to beg him to stay inside where he'd be safe from any retribution by that man Sims. But she couldn't. He wasn't the sort of man to run from trouble. It wouldn't do any good to nag him. He was going to do what he needed to do, whether or not it pleased her.

She got the girls ready for bed and tucked them in. She read them a Dr. Seuss book they hadn't heard yet. When they grew drowsy, she pulled the covers over them and tiptoed to the door, pausing to flick off the light switch as she went out into the hall.

She left the door cracked and went on down the hall to her own room. She got ready for bed and curled up on her pillows with a worn copy of Tacitus' *The Histories*. "I wonder if you ever imagined that people in the future would still be reading words you wrote almost two thousand years ago," she murmured as she thumbed through the well-read work. "And nothing really changes, does it, except the clothes and the everyday things. People are the same."

Her heart wasn't in the book. She laid it aside and turned off the lights, thinking how it would have been two thousand years ago to watch her husband put on his armor and march off to a war in some foreign country behind one of the Roman generals. That made her think of Gil and she gnawed her lip as she lay in the darkness, waiting for some sound that would tell her he was still all right.

It was two o'clock in the morning before she heard a pickup truck pull up at the bottom of the steps out front. She threw off the covers and ran to the window, peering out through the lacy curtain just in time to see Gil and John climb wearily out of the truck. John had a rifle with the breech open under one arm. He led the way into the house, with Gil following behind.

At least, thank God, they were both still alive, she thought. She went back to bed and pulled the covers up to her chin. Relieved, she slept.

She'd forgotten John's invitation to the movies, but he hadn't. And he looked odd, as if he was pondering something wicked, when he waited for her to come down the stairs with the girls.

Kasie was wearing a pretty dark green silk pantsuit with strappy sandals and her hair around her shoulders. She smiled at the little girls in their skirt sets. They looked like a family, and John was touched. He went forward to greet them, pausing to kiss Kasie's cheek warmly.

Gil, who was working in the office, came into the hall just in time to see his brother kissing Kasie. His eyes splintered with unexpected helpless rage. His fists clenched at his side. She wouldn't leave the house with him, but here she was dressed to the nines and all eager to jump into a car with his brother.

John glanced at him warily and hid a smile. "We're off to the movies! Want to come?"

"No," Gil said abruptly. He avoided looking at Kasie. "I've got two more hours of work to finish in the den."

"Let Miss Parsons do it and come with us," John persisted.

"I gave Miss Parsons the day off. She's visiting a friend."

"Let it wait until tomorrow, then."

"No chance. Go ahead and enjoy yourselves, but don't get too comfortable. Watch your back," he said tersely, and returned into the study. He closed the door firmly behind him.

John, for some ungodly reason, was rubbing his hands together with absolute glee. Kasie gave him a speaking glance, which he ignored as he herded them out into the night.

The movie was one for general audiences, about a famous singer. John didn't really enjoy it, but Kasie and the girls did. They ate popcorn and giggled at the funny scenes, and moaned when the heroine was misjudged by the hero and thrown out on her ear.

"That looks familiar, doesn't it?" John murmured outrageously.

"She should hit him with a brickbat," Kasie muttered.

"With a head that hard, I don't know if it would do any good," he said, and Kasie thought for a minute that it didn't sound as if he were referring to the movie. "But I have a much better idea, anyway. Wait and see."

She pondered that enigmatic remark all through the movie. They went home, had dinner and watched TV, but it wasn't until the girls went up to bed and the study door opened that Kasie began to realize what John was up to. Because he waited until his brother had an unobstructed view of the two of them at the foot of the staircase. And then he bent and kissed Kasie. Passionately.

Kasie was shocked. Gil was infuriated. John winked at Kasie before he turned to face his brother. "Oh, there you are," he told Gil with a grin. "The movie was great. I'll tell you all about it tomorrow. Sleep well, Kasie," he added, ruffling the hair at her temple.

"You, too," she choked. She could barely manage words. John had never touched her before, and she knew that it hadn't been out of misplaced passion or raging desire that he'd kissed her. He'd obviously done it to irritate his big brother. And it was working! Gil looked as if he wanted to bite somebody.

He moved close to Kasie when John was out of sight up the steps, whipping out a snow-white handkerchief. He caught her by the nape and wiped off her smeared lipstick.

"You aren't marrying my brother," he said through his teeth.

"Excuse me?"

"I said, you aren't marrying John," he repeated

harshly. "You're an employee here, and that's all. I am not going to let my brother become your meal ticket!"

She actually gasped. "Of all the unfounded, unreasonable, outrageous things in the world to say to a woman, that really takes the cake!" she raged.

"I haven't started yet," he bit off. He threw the handkerchief down on the hall table and pulled her roughly into his arms. "I've never wanted to hit a man so badly in all my life," he ground out as his mouth went down over hers.

She couldn't breathe. He didn't seem to notice, or care. His mouth was warm, hard, insistent. She clung to his shirtfront and let the sensations wash over her like fire. He was insulting her. She shouldn't let him. She should make him stop. It was just that his mouth was so sweet, so masterful, so ardent. She moaned as the sensations piled up on themselves and left her knees wobbling out from under her.

He caught her closer and lifted her against him, devouring her mouth with his own. She felt her whole body begin to shiver with the strength of the desire he was teaching her to feel. Never in her life had she known such pleasure, but even the hungry force of the kiss still wasn't enough to ease the ache in her.

Her arms went up and around his neck and she held on as if she might die by letting go. He groaned huskily as his body began to harden. He wanted her. He wanted to lay her down on the Persian carpet, make passionate love to her. He wanted . . .

He dragged his mouth from hers and looked down at her with accusation and raging anger.

"I'm mad," he growled off. "You aren't supposed to enjoy it."

"Okay," she murmured, trying to coax his mouth back down onto hers. She had no will, no pride, no reason left. She only wanted the pleasure to continue. "Come back here. I'll pretend to hate it."

"Kasie . . ."

She found his mouth and groaned hoarsely as he gave in to his own hunger and crushed her against the length of his tall, fit body. It was the most glorious kiss of her entire life. If only it would never end . . .

But it did, all too soon, and he shot away from her as if he'd tasted poison. His eyes glittered. "If you ever let him kiss you again, I'll throw both of you out a window!"

She opened her mouth to speak, but before she could manage words, the front doorbell rang.

It was one of the cowboys. Two more head of cattle had been shot, and the gunman was still out near the line cabin. One of the cowboys had him pinned down with rifle fire and needed reinforcements. It took Gil precisely five minutes to call John, load his Winchester and get out the door. He barely took time to caution Kasie about venturing outside until the situation was under control. She didn't even get a chance to beg him to be careful. She went upstairs, so that she'd be near the girls, but she knew that this was one night she wouldn't sleep a wink.

Chapter 11

Kasie lay awake for the rest of the night. When dawn broke, she still hadn't heard Gil come into the house. And once she'd thought she heard a shot being fired. Remembering how dangerous the man Sims was supposed to be made her even more uneasy. What if Gil had been shot? How would she live? She couldn't bear the thought of a world without Gil in it.

She got up and dressed just as Mrs. Charters went into the kitchen to start breakfast. John and Gil were nowhere in sight.

"Have they come in at all?" she asked Mrs. Charters.

"Not yet," the older woman said, and looked worried. "There were police cars and sheriff's cars all over the place about two hours ago," she added. "I saw them from my house."

"I thought I heard a shot, but I didn't see anything," Kasie said, and then she really worried.

"You couldn't have seen them, it was three miles and more down the road. But I'm sure we'd have heard if anything had happened to Gil or John."

"Oh, I hope so," Kasie said fervently.

"I'll make coffee," she said. "You can have some in a minute."

"Thanks, Mrs. Charters. I'm going to go sit on the front porch."

"You do that, dear."

The ranch was most beautiful early in the morning, Kasie thought, when dawn broke on the horizon and the cattle and horses started moving around in the pastures. She loved this part of the day, but now it was torment to sit and wonder and not be able to do anything. Had they found Sims? Was he in custody or still at large? And, most frightening of all, was the memory of that single gunshot. Had Gil been hurt?

She nibbled at her fingernails in her nervousness, a habit left over from childhood. There didn't seem to be a vehicle in the world. The highway was close enough that the sound of moving vehicles could be heard very faintly, but at this hour there was very little traffic. In fact, there was none.

She got up from the porch swing and paced restlessly. What if Gil had been shot? Surely someone would have phoned. John would, she was certain. But what if the wound was serious, so serious that he couldn't leave his brother's side even long enough to make a phone call? What if . . . !

The sound of a truck coming down the long ranch road caught her attention. She ran to the top of the steps and stood there with her heart pounding like mad. It was one of the ranch's pickup trucks. She recognized it. Two men were in the cab. They were in a flaming rush. Was it John and one of the hands, come to tell her that Gil was hurt, wounded, dying?

Dust flew as the driver pulled up sharply at the front steps. Both doors flew open. Kasie thought she might faint. John got out of the passenger side, whole and undamaged and grinning. Gil got out on the other side, dusty and worn, with a cut bleeding beside his mouth. But he was all in one piece, not injured, not shot, not . . .

"Gil!" She screamed his name, blind and deaf and dumb to the rest of the world as she came out of her frozen trance and dashed down the steps, missing the bottom one entirely, to rush right into his arms.

"Kasie . . ." He couldn't talk at all, because she was kissing him, blindly, fervently, as if he'd just come back from the dead.

He stopped trying to talk. He kissed her back, his arms enfolding her so closely that her feet dangled while he answered the aching hunger of her mouth.

She was shaking when he lifted his head. His eyes were glittery with feeling as he searched her eyes and saw every single emotion in her. She loved him. She couldn't have told him any plainer if she'd shouted it.

John just chuckled. "I'll go drink coffee while you two . . . talk," he murmured dryly, bypassing them without a backward glance.

Neither of them heard him or saw him go. They stared at each other with aching tenderness, touching faces, lips, fingertips.

"I'm all right," he whispered, kissing her again. "Sims took a shot at us, but he missed. It took two sheriff's deputies, the bloodhounds and a few ranch hands, but we tracked him down. He's in jail, nursing his bruises."

She traced the dried blood on his cheek. "He hit you."

He shrugged. "I hit him, too." He smiled outrageously. "So much for pretending that you only work for me, Kasie," he said with deliberate mischief in his tone.

She touched his dusty hair. "I love you," she said huskily. Her eyes searched his. "Is it all right?"

"That depends," he mused, bending to kiss her gently. "We discussed being old-fashioned, remember?"

She flushed. "I wasn't suggesting . . ."

He took her soft upper lip in both of his and nibbled it. "This is the last place in the world that you and I could carry on a torrid affair," he pointed out. "The girls can take off doorknobs if they have the right tools, and Mrs. Charters probably has microphones and hidden cameras in every room. She always knows whatever's going on around here." He lifted his head and searched her eyes. "I'm glad you love children, Kasie. I really don't plan to stop at Bess and Jenny."

She flushed softly. "Really?"

"We should have one or two of our own," he added quietly. "Boys run in my family, even if Darlene and I were never able to have one. If we had a son or two, it would give Bess and Jenny a chance to be part of a big family."

Her eyes grew dreamy. "We could teach all of them how to use the computer and love cattle."

He smiled tenderly. "But first, I think we might get married," he whispered at her lips. "So that your aunt doesn't have to be embarrassed when she tells people what you're doing."

"We wouldn't want to embarrass Mama Luke," she agreed, bubbling over with joy.

"God forbid," he murmured. He kissed her again, with muted passion. "She can come to the wedding." He hesitated and his eyes darkened. "I'm not sure about my brother. I could have decked him for kissing you!"

"I still don't know why he did," she began.

He chuckled. "He told me. He wanted to see if I was jealous of you. I gave him hell all night until Sims showed up. He laughed all the way back to the ranch. So much for lighting fires under people," he added with a faint grin. "I'll let him be best man, I guess, but he's going to be the only man in church who doesn't get to kiss the bride!"

She laughed. "What a wicked family I'm marrying into," she said as she reached up to kiss him. "And speaking of wicked, we have to invite K.C.," she added shyly.

He froze, lifting his head. "I don't know about that, Kasie . . ."

"You'll like him. Really you will," she promised, smiling widely.

He grimaced. "I suppose we each have to have at least one handicap," he muttered. "I have a lunatic brother and you're best friends with a hit man."

"He's not. You'll like him," she repeated, and drew his head down to hers again. She kissed him with enthusiasm, enjoying the warm, wise tutoring of his hard mouth. "We should go and tell the babies," she whispered against his mouth.

"No need," he murmured.

"Uncle John, look! Daddy's kissing Kasie!"

"See?" he added with a grin as he lifted his head and indicated the front door. Standing there, grinning also, were John, Bess, Jenny, Mrs. Charters, and Miss Parsons.

The wedding was the social event of Medicine Ridge for the summer. Kasie wore a beautiful white gown with lace and a keyhole necklace, with a Juliet cap and a long veil. She looked, Gil whispered as she joined him at the altar, like an angel.

Her excited eyes approved his neat gray vested suit, which made his hair look even more blond. At either side of them were Bess and Jenny in matching blue dresses, carrying baskets of white roses. Next to them was John, his brother's best man, fumbling in his pocket for the wedding rings he was responsible for.

As the ceremony progressed, a tall, blond man in the front pew watched with narrowed, wistful eyes as his godchild married the eldest of the Callister heirs. Not bad, K.C. Kantor thought, for a girl who'd barely survived a military uprising even before she was born. He glanced at the woman seated next to him, his eyes sad and quiet, as he contemplated what might have been if he'd met Kasie's aunt before her heart led her to a life of service in a religious order. They were the best of friends and they corresponded. She would always be family to him. She was the only family he had, or would ever have, except for that sweet young woman at the altar.

"Isn't she beautiful?" Mama Luke whispered to him.

"A real vision," he agreed.

She smiled at him with warm affection and turned her attention back to the ceremony.

As the priest pronounced them man and wife, Gil lifted the veil and bent to kiss Kasie. There were sighs all around, until a small hand tugged hard at Kasie's skirt and a little voice was heard asking plaintively, "Is it over yet, Daddy? I have to go to the bathroom!"

Later, laughing about the small interruption as they gathered in the fellowship hall of the church, Kasie and Gil each cuddled a little girl and fed them cake.

"It was nice of Pauline to apologize for what she did in the Bahamas," Kasie murmured, recalling the telephone call that had both surprised and pleased her the day before the ceremony.

"She's really not that bad," Gil mused. "Just irresponsible and possessive. But I still didn't want her at the wedding," he added with a grin. "Just in case."

"I still wish you'd invited your parents," Kasie told Gil gently.

"I did," he replied. "They were on their way to the Bahamas and couldn't spare the time." He smiled at her. "Don't worry the subject, Kasie. Some things can't be changed. We're a family, you and me and the girls and John."

"Yes, we are," she agreed, and she reached up to

kiss him. She glanced around them curiously. Mama Luke intercepted the glance and joined them.

"He left as we were coming in here," she told Kasie. "K.C. never was one for socializing. I expect he's headed for the airport by now."

"It was nice of him to come."

"It was," she agreed. She handed a small box to Kasie. "He asked me to give this to you."

She frowned, pausing to open the box. She drew out a gold necklace with a tiny crystal ball dangling from it. Inside the ball was a tiny seed.

"It's a mustard seed," Mama Luke explained. "It's from a Biblical quote—if you have even that amount of faith, as a mustard seed, nothing is impossible. It's to remind you that miracles happen."

Kasie cradled it in her hand and looked up at Gil with her heart in her eyes. "Indeed they do," she whispered, and all the love she had for her new husband was in her face.

The next night, Kasie and Gil lay tangled in a king-size bed at a rented villa in Nassau, exhausted and deliciously relaxed from their first intimacy.

Kasie moved shyly against him, her face flushed in the aftermath of more physical sensation than she'd ever experienced.

"Stop that," he murmured drowsily. "I'm useless now. Go to sleep."

She laughed with pure delight and curled closer. "All right. But don't forget where we left off."

He drew her closer. "As if I could!" He bent and

kissed her eyes shut. "Kasie, I never dreamed that I could be this happy again." His eyes opened and looked into hers with fervent possession. "I loved Darlene. A part of me will always love her. But I would die for you," he added roughly, his eyes blazing with emotion.

Overwhelmed, she buried her face in his throat and shivered. "I would die for you," she choked. She clung harder. "I love you!"

His mouth found hers, hungry for contact, for the sharing of fierce, exquisite need. He drew her over his relaxed body and held her until the trembling stopped. His breath sighed out heavily at her ear. "Forever, Kasie," he whispered unsteadily.

She smiled. "Forever."

They slept, eventually, and as dawn filtered in through the venetian blinds and the sound of the surf grew louder, there was a knock on the door.

Gil opened his eyes, still drowsy. He looked down at Kasie, fast asleep on her stomach, smiling even so. He smiled, too, and tossed the sheet over her before he stepped into his Bermuda shorts and went to answer the door.

The shock when he opened it was blatant. On the doorstep were a silver-haired man in casual slacks and designer shirt, and a silver-haired woman in a neat but casual sundress and overblouse. They were carrying the biggest bouquet of orchids Gil had ever seen in his life.

The man pushed the bouquet toward Gil hesitantly

and with a smile that seemed both hesitant and uncertain. "Congratulations," he said.

"From both of us," the woman added.

They both stood there, waiting.

As Gil searched for words, there was movement behind him and Kasie came to the door in the flowered cotton muu-muu she'd bought for the trip, her long chestnut hair disheveled, smiling broadly.

"Hello!" she exclaimed, going past Gil to hug the woman and then the man, who both flushed. "I'm so glad you could come!"

Gil stared at her. "What?"

"I phoned them," she told him, clasping his big hand in hers. "They said they'd like to come over and have lunch with us, and I told them to come today. But I overslept," she added, and flushed.

"It's your honeymoon, you should oversleep," Gil's mother, Magdalene, said gently. She looked at her son nervously. "We wanted to come to the wedding," she said. "But we didn't want to, well, ruin the day for you."

"That's right," Jack Callister agreed gruffly. "We haven't been good parents. At first we were too irresponsible, and then we were too ashamed. Especially when Douglas took you in and we lost touch." He shrugged. "It's too late to start over, of course, but we'd sort of like to, well, to get to know you and John. And the girls, of course. That is, if you, uh, if you . . ." He shrugged.

Kasie squeezed Gil's hand, hard.

"I'd like that," he said obligingly.

Their faces changed. They beamed. For several seconds, they looked like silver-haired children on Christmas morning. And Gil realized with stark shock that they were just that—grown-up children without the first idea of how to be parents. Douglas Callister had kept the boys, and he hadn't approved of his brother Jack, so he hadn't encouraged contact. Since the elder Callisters didn't know how to approach their children directly, they lost touch and then couldn't find a way to reach them at all.

He looked down at Kasie, and it all made sense. She'd tied the loose ends up. She'd gathered a family back together.

She squeezed Gil's hand again, looking up at him with radiant delight. "We could get dressed and meet them in the restaurant. After we put these in water," she added, hugging the bouquet to her heart and sniffing them. "I've never had orchids in my life," she said with a smile. "Thank you!"

Magdalena laughed nervously. "No, Kasie. Thank *you*."

"We'll get dressed and meet you in about fifteen minutes, in the restaurant," Gil managed to say.

"Great!" Jack said. He took his wife's hand, and they both smiled, looking ten years younger. "We'll see you there!"

The door closed and Gil looked down at Kasie with wonder.

"I thought they might like to visit us at the ranch next month, too," Kasie said, "so they can get to know the babies."

189

"You're amazing," he said. "Absolutely amazing!"

She fingered the necklace K.C. had given her at the wedding. "I like miracles, don't you?"

He burst out laughing. He picked her up and swung her around in an arc while she squealed and held on to her bouquet tightly. He put her down gently and kissed her roughly.

"I love you," he said huskily.

She grinned. "Yes, and see what it gets you when you love people? You get all sorts of nice surprises. In fact," she added with a mischievous grin, "I have all sorts of surprises in store for you."

He took a deep breath and looked at her with warm affection. "I can hardly wait."

She kissed him gently and went to dress. She gave a thought to Gil's Darlene, and to her own parents, and her lost twin and his family, and hoped that they all knew, somehow, that she and Gil were happy and that they had a bright future with the two little girls and the children they would have together. As she went to the closet to get her dress, her eyes were full of dreams. And so were Gil's.

Center Point Publishing
600 Brooks Road ● PO Box 1
Thorndike ME 04986-0001 USA

(207) 568-3717

US & Canada:
1 800 929-9108